She'd show him

Sex panther was more like it.

Growling under her breath, she headed for the hotel elevator. She had splurged on a manicure, pedicure and a facial. She'd shaved her legs, plucked her eyebrows and waxed her upper lip. She was smooth and pampered and sleekly groomed. Tonight Eden was an overworked Manhattan CEO in a black bustier with a garter and thigh-high stockings on underneath her staid gray business suit—an executive who liked tying men up and having her way with them.

And Alec would be the one.

By the time he knocked on the door, Eden had music playing, candles flickering and the champagne uncorked. When she opened the door, he bounded inside and swept her into his arms.

"God," he groaned, "I thought tonight would never get here. The waiting kills me."

"Ah," Eden replied, "that's part of my plan."

"Your plan is more evil than world domination."

"Ha. You'll think evil when you find out what I have in store for you tonight."

"Bring it on," he said, a smile searing his lips.

Blaze™

Dear Reader,

One day when I was cleaning my house—yes, even we Blaze authors must put down the sex toys occasionally and dust cobwebs—a snippet of provocative dialogue popped into my head. I had no idea who the characters were or the premise of the story, just the opening conversation.

However, it didn't take me long to realize I had a powerful theme to explore. What holds a woman back from acting out her most seductive sexual fantasies? Once I asked that question, Eden Montgomery began to whisper her story into my ear. And when I learned Eden's secret shame I knew she needed someone tender and caring. Someone fun loving and spontaneous and just a little bit reckless. Someone who would encourage her to face her fears and embrace her sexuality. Someone like daredevil Alec Ramsey.

Except, with the help of her friends and a very special stone, Eden ends up teaching Alec far more about love than he ever bargained for. I hope you enjoy Eden and Alec's story and that your own romantic adventures are, well…wickedly wonderful.

I love to hear from my readers. You can visit my Web site www.loriwilde.com or write to me at loriwilde02@yahoo.com.

Lori Wilde

Books by Lori Wilde

HARLEQUIN BLAZE
30—A TOUCH OF SILK
66—A THRILL TO REMEMBER

PACKED WITH PLEASURE

Lori Wilde

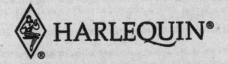

HARLEQUIN®

TORONTO • NEW YORK • LONDON
AMSTERDAM • PARIS • SYDNEY • HAMBURG
STOCKHOLM • ATHENS • TOKYO • MILAN • MADRID
PRAGUE • WARSAW • BUDAPEST • AUCKLAND

To Diana Tidlund
A very special woman who makes the world a better place.

ISBN 0-373-79110-0

PACKED WITH PLEASURE

Copyright © 2003 by Laurie Vanzura.

1

"Red-velvet-lined handcuffs?"

"Check."

"Silk blindfold?"

"Check."

"Crotchless crimson lace panties?"

"Check."

"Cinnamon-scented massage oil?"

"Check."

"Video camera and extra cassettes?"

"Check and double check."

"Plenty of condoms?"

Eden Montgomery clicked her tongue and shot her petite, purple-and-scarlet-haired assistant a chiding glance. "Ashley, I'm a professional. Of course I've included condoms."

"Hey," Ashley protested, waving a tattooed wrist. "I'm just trying to keep you out of trouble."

"What do you mean?" Eden frowned. "Trouble?"

Ashley cleared her throat. "Well, I didn't really want to say anything because this was a rush order, but you do realize that you created this exact same gift basket a couple of months ago? Back then, I think you called it Seduction in Scarlet."

Eden stared at her assistant, and then shifted her gaze to the basket. A lump of dismay slid down her throat. Good grief, Ashley was right. The basket was identical to one she'd made for a famous Broadway actor's thirty-fifth birthday. Right down to the vermilion pashmina she'd used to line the basket.

"Don't look so stricken. Repeating yourself is no great tragedy, even if you *do* advertise your baskets as one-of-a-kind creations. Seriously, E., who's gonna know?"

"I'll know." Immediately, Eden began dismantling the basket, tossing items out across the counter. Her reputation was based on her word. She would not be guilty of false advertising.

"Look, you don't have time for a major overhaul. The customer is due to pick it up this afternoon."

"I don't care."

"What are you going to do instead?"

"I don't know." Eden looked at the demolished basket, the urge to cry surprising her with its intensity.

"Admit it, you *have* been rather frazzled for the past month or so," Ashley observed. "What you need is a good long vacation."

Frazzled wasn't the word for it. Lately, she had been well…stagnant.

As the proprietor of Wickedly Wonderful, a tiny boutique in a trendy slice of Manhattan that specialized in erotic gift baskets for those uniquely seductive occasions such as honeymoons and anniversaries, Eden's business lived or died on the strength of her creativity. Unfortunately, her artistic fount had run dry.

She had slammed headlong into an invisible mental wall. She was blocked. Clogged. Bereft of an original concept.

The thrill was gone.

Think. Come on, Eden, you can do it. Come up with a fresh idea.

She couldn't really pinpoint when she'd started to lose intimacy with her work, but about five weeks ago, almost two years to the day after the tragic fiery accident that had led her to specializing in erotica, she'd noticed her concentration slipping. Before the fire she had operated a normal gift store, producing baskets for all occasion from holidays to bar mitzvahs to baby showers, but she'd had difficulty keeping the business solvent.

And then two things had happened. One, a regular client had asked her to design an erotic gift basket for her sister's honeymoon and, two, Eden's apartment building had caught fire.

She'd helped her elderly neighbor, Mrs. Grant, escape, but she'd then gone back into the building to help others. A burning ceiling beam had fallen, pinning her pelvis to the floor. Two burly members of the FDNY had arrived just in time to save her from succumbing to smoke inhalation. They hadn't, however, been able to stop her from receiving third-degree burns.

Eden briefly closed her eyes, sucked in her breath and grimaced at the remembered pain of the fateful night that had changed her life forever. Involuntarily, she splayed a palm across her lower abdomen.

"Is there something going on?" Ashley angled her head. The tiny hoop earring pierced through her left eyebrow caught the light and glinted gold. "Do you want to talk about it?"

"Not really," she denied. Usually people confided in her, not the other way around. She was more comfortable being the shoulder to cry on than the one revealing her feelings.

"Does it have anything to do with the fire?"

Eden shot her a look. Ashley was much more perceptive than most people gave her credit for. Her flibbertigibbet personality gave the impression of someone too mercurial for deep thoughts.

"Why would you suppose that?"

"Because every time you think about the fire you touch your scar."

Immediately, Eden jerked her hand from her abdomen. She'd had reconstructive surgery last summer and the scars were much less noticeable now. She needed to stop focusing on her wounds. Not so easy to do when the burns were indirectly related to her current creative slump.

Following the fire, a prominent newspaper had done a feature piece on her, lauding her as a hero. She'd felt awkward with the title and uncomfortable with the attention. She'd only done what anyone else would have done in the same situation.

A reporter and her cameraman had come to the shop and spied the sexy basket Eden had started con-cocting for her client, but hadn't completed before the fire put her out of commission. The reporter had honed in on that basket and enthusiastically touted Eden as the Renoir of erotic gift basket design.

After the article came out, Eden's phone had rung off the hook with orders. Business mushroomed. She renamed the store, changing it from Hildy's Hideaway to Wickedly Wonderful. Her financial woes vanished, but she had felt like a fraud. She knew next to nothing about the sexual adventures she created in her baskets beyond her own vivid imagination.

To counter her feelings of inadequacy, she'd studied every sex manual and erotic book she could lay her hands on. From the Kama Sutra to *The Story of O*. Her newly acquired but totally academic knowledge of sex, combined with her degree in art history from N.Y.U., had stimulated her efforts.

And for a while it had been great fun, living vicariously through her work. She loved mentally exploring the tempting fantasies she'd never gotten to experience in the flesh.

To date, she'd only had one lover. Harry Jackson, an old college friend she'd trusted but had never been particularly aroused by. She'd decided to lose her virginity at twenty calmly and rationally, unclouded by complicated passion.

She'd experienced enough chaos and drama in her upbringing and she'd been determined to keep her feet on the ground when it came to romantic encounters. She refused to end up like her flighty mother, bouncing from one lover to another always on the lookout for the heady high of a new relationship but never staying with any one of them long enough to learn the deeper pleasure of a meaningful commitment.

She and Harry had made a pact to deflower each other and poor Harry had been as inept as she. Their fumbling attempts at lovemaking were a clear-cut case of the virginal leading the virginal with neither one of them experiencing fireworks. But then again, neither one of them had gotten hurt, either, and that had been the entire point.

Now, she sort of regretted missing out on the crazy tumult of first lust—it might have kept her imagination fueled. But she was a consummate professional and very adept at hiding her lack of personal knowledge. Her limited sexual experience was a closely guarded secret. After all, who would buy erotic gift baskets from a woman with a nonexistent sex life?

Snap out of it, she scolded herself and furrowed her brow, probing the depths of her mind for even a whisper of a sensual fantasy, but she drew a complete blank.

She was officially tapped out. Empty. Drained.

Imagine a handsome, sexy guy.

Closing her eyes, she waited for a flash of insight. Nothing.

Oh come on, visualize some sex-god movie star.

Zero.

Eden could not dredge up a single person who popped her cork.

Panic ripped through her then and she rhythmically

worried red cellophane wrapping paper between her fingers. Her fussbudget mind snatched up the fear and sprinted with it, spinning a hundred what-if situations.

What if she never felt sexy again? What if she couldn't break this block? What if business dwindled? What if she had to let Ashley go? What if she lost the store her grandmother Hildy had owned for forty years before Eden had inherited it?

Worst-case scenario? She would end up a bag lady on the street, pushing a grocery cart of discarded rubbish she'd gleaned from trash Dumpsters and mumbling crazily to herself.

Her eyes flew open. What was she going to do?

"Don't start imagining some huge tragedy over this," Ashley said. "Let's just replace everything that's red with black and call it Midnight Memories."

"But the customer wanted red."

"Then just change a few things. Instead of the pashmina, use a satin teddy. Replace the handcuffs with ropes. Instead of massage oil, go for body paints or edible panties."

"That's not part of the artistic vision."

"Well, the artistic vision you came up with was a rerun. Either ditch the lofty standards or be happy with a duplicate."

"You're right. Let's do it your way."

They worked silently for a few minutes, exchanging and rearranging items and then Ashley ventured, "Are you *sure* you don't want to talk?"

Ashley was a sweetheart, but Eden couldn't see unburdening herself to the free-spirited nineteen-year-old even though the young woman probably knew way more about sex than Eden did and she was six years younger. Ashley's advice was bound to be something wild and crazy. Like have a red-hot fling with a handsome stranger.

Well, she'd tried that, hadn't she? Her one miserable attempt at reconnecting with her femininity had ended in terrible failure when Josh Cameron—a guy she'd known only a couple of weeks before going to bed with him—had been so repulsed by her burns he'd fled her apartment without having sex with her.

That kind of reaction didn't do a hell of a lot for a girl's self-esteem.

Eden clenched a red satin bow in her hand and sank her top front teeth into her bottom lip to eradicate the memory of her single pathetic attempt at having intercourse after she'd been burned. In the wake of Josh's reaction she'd been too scared of rejection to try again.

"Do you wanna know why I think you're so frazzled?" Ashley asked.

Please save me from the wisdom of teenagers.

"Not really."

"You need to get some juicy booty."

"Ashley!"

"Don't go all prude on me. If I'm not mistaken that's a man-shaped vibrator you're holding. Seriously, I think that's why your baskets have been a bit blah lately. You need a little divine inspiration."

"Thanks for your opinion. I'll take it under consideration."

"I know this hot-looking spray-paint artist who specializes in nudes. I think you two would really hit it off."

"I can find my own dates, thank you."

"Hmm. I've been working here almost ten months and as far as I know you haven't hooked up with a guy even once. You spend all your time building fantasies and no time living them. Under those conditions anyone would burn out."

"I appreciate your concern, but my love life is my private business. Could we talk about something else, please?"

Ashley shrugged. "Suit yourself."

At that moment the wind chimes over the door whispered a resonant woodsy sound and a shapely older woman dressed in the latest designer fall fashions stepped over the threshold.

The woman was Jayne Lockerbee. Her favorite customer. Eden smiled.

Jayne was one red-hot granny who believed sex should be discussed freely and enjoyed often. She loved shocking her conservative friends and relatives by gifting them with Eden's baskets.

"Yo, J. Lo!" Ashley greeted Jayne in the hip, breezy style Eden so often envied.

"Hey, Ash, what's happenin'?" Mrs. Lockerbee grinned.

"Not much. How's Mr. Lo?"

"Sexy as ever." The woman winked. "In fact,

that's why I'm here. I need a very special gift basket for our thirtieth wedding anniversary.''

''No kidding? That's so awesome. Married thirty years and you're still having wild sex,'' Ashley blurted.

''Better than ever. There's nothing sexier than experience.'' Mrs. Lockerbee turned her attention to Eden. ''Now about that basket. I was thinking maybe a little Tarzan and Jane action. What can you create for me along those lines?''

''I'll help her, if you wanna finish that.'' Ashley nodded.

Normally Eden handled all gift consultations, but Ashley knew Jayne well and she was trying to help out in the face of Eden's creative crash and burn.

''Sure. That'll be fine.''

''Really?'' Ashley's eyes lit up at the honor Eden had bestowed upon her.

''Really. You don't mind if Ashley waits on you this time, do you, Jayne?''

''Of course not. Maybe Ashley will even share some of her sexual escapades with me.'' Jayne winked. ''I haven't forgotten what it's like to be young.''

Have I? Eden thought. The notion was an unsettling one. Old before her time. Washed-up before she'd ever really started living.

''We just got in these great new leopard-print loincloths,'' Ashley said to Jayne.

''Hmm, sounds promising.''

"Here, let me show you." Ashley escorted Jayne to the rear of the store.

Shaking the doubt from her head, Eden returned to the task at hand. What would it be like to have Jayne's life? Married thirty years and still enjoying terrific sex. Would she ever have that?

With those scars? Not likely.

Eden sighed. Some people were lucky in love. Apparently, she was not. On that score, she was her mother's daughter.

But it doesn't mean you can't be lucky in lust, nudged a naughty voice at the back of her mind. *Come on, Eden, you know you want to have sex.*

And expanding her sexual horizons *would* be good for both business and her creativity. It was the missing piece of the puzzle and in her heart she knew it.

Her cautious nature had held her back for too long. Lack of experience was what had her feeling like a fraud, and feeling like a fraud was responsible for her artistic block.

And just because Josh was a jerk didn't mean all men would run away at the sight of her scars. She just had to take her time and find a kind, sensitive lover who intimately knew his way around a woman's body. Simply entertaining thoughts of that mystery lover had her tingling with longing.

Okay, all right. She needed to get laid. But even if she was willing to take a huge risk, strip off her clothes in front of a stranger and reveal her secret vulnerability, she had absolutely no prospects in mind—Ashley's hottie spray-paint artist aside.

She tied the big red bow around the basket and then stepped over to place it in the orders-waiting-to-be-picked-up glass display case. She set the basket down, and then slowly raised her head and peered out the front window that was open just a crack.

The air hung heavy with the rich scent of impending rain. Humidity-laden wind gusted, sending a swirl of fallen leaves gathering along the curb.

It was the sort of enigmatic, electrically charged afternoon that lingered between dwindling summer and impending autumn that stirred a woman's blood and made her believe in the endless possibilities of titillating encounters with dark fantasy men.

That's when she saw him. Standing rooted to the sidewalk, looking as if he owned the entire street while everyone else scurried around him.

Inexplicably, she sucked in her breath and a shiver of anticipation scampered down her spine.

God, he was gorgeous. Skyscraper tall and daredevil muscular, his lush dark hair curled to his collar giving him a wild, roguish appearance in spite of his tailored pinstriped business suit. His face was lean and chiseled, his mouth full and tempting. His eyes were the smoky-gray of a grass fire and fringed with black lashes dense as paintbrushes.

He was the sort of man who made even a reticent woman itch to get naked. Ambushed by this totally unexpected and intense attraction, Eden's knees weakened as a dozen forbidden images tumbled through her brain.

What was happening here? Just minutes ago she'd

been unable to dredge up a single sexual fantasy and now she couldn't stop them.

She pictured herself rolling around on a heart-shaped bed in a woodsy cabin in the Catskills with the guy. She imagined their sweaty bodies pressed together as they made love on the floor of a grass hut in Bora Bora. She envisioned them grinding against each other on a bearskin rug before a roaring fireplace in Iceland.

He was a plundering pirate and she was his captive. She was a streetwalker plying her trade and he was her randy john. He was a virile gunslinger and she was the timid schoolmarm come to teach in his untamed town.

She tasted the briny flavor of his skin as she bit his bare shoulder. She inhaled the smell of coconut, bananas and lusty man. She heard his deep-throated groan as he called out her name in the ecstasy of climax.

Omigod, omigod, omigod.

Stunned and excited, Eden raised a hand to her throat. The magic was back.

And then he leveled his gaze, stared straight through the window at her and started into the store.

2

ALEC RAMSEY DOUBLE-CHECKED the Soho address on the slip of paper in his pocket. Yep, Wickedly Wonderful, this was the place his oldest sister Sarah had recommended.

He raised his head and started to move toward the door, but then his eyes landed on the woman in the storefront window and he froze.

Spellbound, he simply stared. She was leaning over, placing something in the window and oh, so slightly exposing just a hint of cleavage. The sight was enough to cause instant sweat to bead on the back of his neck despite the recent drop in temperature.

A burst of wind snatched a red banner from the awning of a nearby building. It sailed down, fluttering in the breeze, until it caught on an updraft just above the storefront window at exactly the same time the woman glanced up.

For a whisper of a second it was a pure Kodak moment. The foxy, heart-faced woman framed by a crimson banner. The effect was mesmerizingly magical. And even after the banner twisted and spiraled away into the wind, Alec couldn't take his eyes off her.

His heart literally skipped a beat and the unexpected arrhythmia startled him. Usually, the only time his pulse skittered was when he bungee-jumped or hang-glided or skydived.

The sun slipped out from behind a cloud where it had been hiding and glinted off her mass of chestnut curls swept back so fetchingly in a loose ponytail. She wore a long-sleeved turquoise peasant blouse. Not exactly high fashion, but it was definitely romantic. His fingers itched to stroke both the tactile material and what lay intriguingly beyond.

He knew the correct terminology for her garment because he had four sisters who had spent their lives telling him about clothes. He owed them a debt of gratitude. The knowledge came in handy with his active dating life. Women were impressed when a heterosexual male could converse intelligently about fashion.

Their gazes met. And locked.

She possessed the most arrestingly blue eyes he'd ever seen.

Alec swallowed. Hard.

She glanced away quickly but then a moment later she was back, eyeing him with slow, deliberate intent until he felt as if he were a job applicant on an interview.

He couldn't get into the shop quickly enough.

Wind chimes murmured a musical note as he pushed through the door. The rousing scent of cinnamon candles filled the small room and everywhere he looked he saw something seductive.

Peacock feathers and skimpy panties and black leather masks. Whips and chains and swatches of sensual fabrics. Erotic videos and vibrators and chocolate body paint.

"May I help you?"

He jerked his head around and came face-to-face with his dream woman. Her name tag read Eden. Ah, a woman who crafted erotic gifts named Eden. How apropos.

She smiled, her small but full mouth lifting dazzlingly at the corners. He was aware of a high, humming sexual energy flowing between them.

Her impact was not the strike of a classic beauty but rather like the welcoming influence of a warm, rich hug. An invisible hug that wrapped around him like an aura—distinct and unmistakably *her*.

She possessed a certain luster that whispered to something deep inside him. Something primal and patently masculine. Something sweetly taboo.

His heart skipped another beat. Amazed at his aberrant reaction, Alec had to clear his throat before he could speak.

"I need…" Damn, how could he think with her studying him like that?

"Yes?" she gently urged, and raised a quizzical eyebrow.

I need. I need. I need.

What did he need? Frowning, Alec ripped his gaze from her lips and met those long-lashed, sky-blue eyes again.

"Um…"

Brilliant, Ramsey, absolutely brilliant. When was the last time a woman had left him tongue-tied? He searched his memory and couldn't think of a single occurrence.

"Did you want to order a gift?" She lifted a hand to push a tendril of hair from her face, the bracelets at her elegant wrist jangled quietly.

"Yes. Yes. That's it."

"And what is the occasion?"

"My business partner, who also happens to be my best friend, is getting married the first Saturday in November."

"You'll be wanting a honeymoon basket."

"Yeah." He nodded.

That's right, dazzle her with your sparkling conversational skills, you suave devil, you.

Irritated with himself, he racked his brain for something else to say. "My sister Sarah Armstrong got married in April and someone gave her one of your baskets as a gift. She said it made the honeymoon."

"Yes. The Ramsey-Armstrong wedding. I believe her basket was called Palm Tree Passion. Were you wanting to order something similar for your friend?"

"Wow," Alec said, impressed. "That's some kind of memory."

"It's a Montgomery family trait," she replied. "Although it often comes in handy when running a business, vividly remembering everything that happened to you can sometimes be a minus."

A brief wistfulness moved across her face and Alec experienced a rush of empathy. There were quite a few things in his life he was glad remained fuzzy. Like his father's fatal heart attack, and the time he busted up his leg during a motorcycle race.

Mentally he shook his head, still unable to believe he'd not only survived but had in fact thrived. He'd come so far. From the scrappy kid who got involved in one daredevil stunt after another as a way of dealing with his father's death to the well-respected editor in chief of a very successful men's magazine. He had gone from borderline poverty to being rich beyond his wildest dreams, and he owed his success to his uncle Mac and the ability to face his fears head-on and defy them.

"My baskets are each original creations," Eden said, breaking into his memory. "Tailor-made for the recipient. Can you tell me a little more about your friend?"

"Randy?" Alec grinned. "He's a hotdogger and a half. A balls-to-the-wall no-fear sort of guy." His grin disappeared. "But he's been different ever since he met Jill."

"Different?"

"You know. He's love-struck. Has this dopey smile on his face all the time. Doesn't want to do the things he used to do."

"His priorities have shifted."

"Yeah," he said nostalgically, already missing their bachelor high jinks. He was happy for Randy, but he knew things would never be the same between them again.

"And what's his fiancée like?"

Alec was incredibly aware of exactly how close they were standing. Eden was near enough to touch. He could feel the very air vibrating between them.

"Jill's nice. Quiet. Not the type I pictured him with."

"And what type is that?"

"Well, Randy is so bold I guess I always imagined him with someone a bit more..." He hesitated.

How to put this so it didn't sound as if he didn't like Jill. He did like her. She was very sweet. Demure, a little shy and very brainy. It's just that he couldn't figure out why this particular woman? How had Randy known that, above all the other women in the world, Jill was the one? His buddy had dated women who were certainly more beautiful, more adventure-some, more sophisticated. Why her? Why now? How was she different from the rest?

"Yes?" Eden prompted.

"Flashy. I pictured him with a colorful, flamboyant woman."

"From what you tell me, Randy seems pretty flam-boyant all on his own."

"He is."

"So maybe opposites attract?"

Their gazes met and that same arc of electricity that had called to him on the street surged again with star-tling clarity. Opposites attract, eh? What about this sudden chemistry between them? They were anything but opposites. A woman who spent her days con-cocting erotic fantasies had to be just as sexually ad-venturous as he.

"Maybe. They're doing this second virginity thing. Personally, I don't get it, but Randy claims they're not having sex until after the wedding to prove their love for each other." He shrugged.

"Randy's newfound celibacy and choice of mates isn't what's really bothering you, is it? It's the simple fact he's getting married."

"Bothering me?" Alec stepped back. "Who says I'm bothered about Randy getting married."

"You're losing your stag partner."

"What?" He blinked at her.

"When Randy got engaged to Jill, you no longer had someone to go chasing babes with. No strip-club buddy. No one with whom to take potshots at married life. Plus, as his business partner you're fretting that his marriage will affect his career choices."

Alec stared, open mouthed. He was taken aback by her insight. How could she know that ever since Randy met Jill he'd felt not only left out but also worried about the future of their business?

It was one thing for two carefree bachelors to publish a magazine called *Single Guy*. It was quite another for one of those bachelors to be shackled in matrimony. Alec feared Randy would forget how to connect with their happily single readership and the magazine would lose its competitive edge.

And secretly, in the dark recesses of his mind, in a place he refused to acknowledge existed, Alec was jealous. Not of married life. Oh, no. He realized that particular institution wasn't for him, but of the special closeness Jill and Randy shared. Seeing them together sometimes made him wonder if indulging in daredevil sports, hopping from trendy nightclub to trendy nightclub, attending lavish parties, and wining and dining local celebrities was all there was to life.

He hated being forced to examine his lifestyle choices.

What he needed in order to shake off this woefully inappropriate "third wheel" feeling was a good old-fashioned fling with a woman who knew lots of naughty bedroom tricks. Indulging in the thrill of the chase never failed to lift his spirits.

And from the looks of this erotic shop and the seethe of sexual chemistry oozing between them, he suspected Eden was exactly the kind of woman he was looking for. And he was already having wickedly wonderful thoughts about how to please her in bed.

She was asking him more questions about Jill and Randy. What kind of fabrics they liked, their favorite movies, their mood music.

But Alec wasn't listening. All he could think about was kissing those luscious lips of hers.

"I had no idea this process was so involved," he said, but he was thinking, *How can I get you into my arms?*

"Oh, yes." She nodded. "When you buy an Eden Montgomery original you're getting much more than sex toys in a basket. You're purchasing a gift of art from the heart as well as a treat for the senses."

Man, did he want to experience her treats firsthand. She was exactly what the doctor ordered. A shot of pure sexual adventure to chase away his "my-best-friend-is-getting-married" blues.

"Sarah did say she'd never seen anything quite like your baskets."

"I must warn you, gift consultation can take as long as an hour."

"No kidding."

"I'm a stickler for details, but you can rest assured your friends will appreciate your gift. I guarantee my work."

A brilliant idea occurred to him. Alec checked his watch. "If the consultation takes an hour then I can't do this today. I've got an appointment in Midtown in forty-five minutes. Plus I don't have all the data you need. How about this—I talk to Randy, find out more about Jill's likes and dislikes." He reached into a pocket for his business card and passed it over to her. "You drop by my office around one tomorrow afternoon, I'll buy you lunch for your trouble and we can do the consultation then. How does that sound?"

Eden accepted his card and stared down at it. She hesitated a moment and his heart did that idiotic beat-skipping thing again.

She's going to say no, he thought, and his spirits plummeted.

What in the hell was the matter with him? He hadn't been this nervous since his high school prom. Blame his uncharacteristic anxiety on a long dry spell.

Speaking of second virginity, he'd been celibate for the past eight months. Not because he hadn't had plenty of opportunities, but simply because no one had excited him to the point of making an effort.

Until now.

She wet her lips with the tip of her tongue then raised her eyes to meet his again.

Thump-thump-thump went his ticker.

"Okay," she said. "Why not?"

SHE HAD A DATE.

For the first time in almost a year she had a date. A date with—Eden stared at the card still clutched in her hand—Alec Ramsey.

The little rectangle of stiff paper burned a hole in her palm, but already the powerful rush of creative sexual energy she had experienced in his presence was starting to dissipate. Had she imagined it all?

Come on, it's not a date, niggled her nay-saying voice. It's a business luncheon.

Before she had time to argue with herself about the "date" versus "not date" status of her appointment with Alec, Ashley and Mrs. Lockerbee pounced.

"Omigod," Ashley clutched her hand to her heart. "Was that guy gorgeous or what?"

"Not only gorgeous," Mrs. Lockerbee said. "But rich and famous, too."

"Famous?" Eden furrowed her brow.

"Don't tell me you didn't recognize him?" Mrs. Lockerbee clicked her tongue.

"That's because you were too busy drooling," Ashley commented. "Not that I blame you one tiny bit. And the cool thing was, he seemed just as taken with you.''

''He didn't.''

''Oh, but he did.'' Ashley nodded knowingly.

''His card just gives his name, business address and phone number. Don't leave me hanging in suspense, Jayne. Who is Alec Ramsey?''

Jayne telegraphed her a wicked smile. ''Why, darling, that perfect specimen of manhood is none other than the publisher of *Single Guy* magazine and the most eligible bachelor in Manhattan.''

''You know him personally?''

''Last year we served on the board of the Kids Count charity together. He's very big into helping underprivileged youths and he really means what he says. He's not just some rich guy throwing money around to boost his public image.''

''I would never have guessed it.'' He looked so sophisticated and polished Eden had a hard time imagining him hanging with street kids.

''Alec lost his own father when he was in his teens, a heart attack I think, and it had a lasting impact on him. He doesn't take anything for granted. That's why he works so hard. I think his earnestness just adds to his sex appeal.''

''I'm meeting him for lunch tomorrow.''

''Get outta here!'' Ashley gave her a playful shove. ''You go, woman.''

''Only to discuss a gift consultation. It's just business.''

"The way you're smiling indicates it's much more than just business." Jayne wagged a knowing finger.

"Okay," Eden confessed, her grin spreading and giddiness flitting through her. "It could be more than business. We'll see."

"This totally rocks," Ashley enthused. "Now maybe you'll have hot sex and get your groove back."

"Hey, hey, don't go jumping to conclusions. I'm simply meeting him for lunch."

Now that Ashley had expressed out loud the thoughts revolving in her head, Eden's prudent side kicked in and a panicky fear gripped her. She wasn't like her freewheeling, irresponsible mother. She could not have a wild affair with a stranger even if he *had* jumped-started her libido and her imagination with a single rakish grin. The fact that she was even considering such a thing tempted her to break the date.

Play it safe. Call him up and tell him you can't meet him. You can do the gift consultation over the phone. No need for a face-to-face.

Ah, now there was the rub. She had been listening to her nay-saying, fussbudget voice for too long. Playing it safe hadn't gotten her anywhere. It was way past time she took a risk, moved from her comfort zone and stepped out of the box.

"Lunch could turn into a little afternoon delight," Ashley ribbed her.

"But I don't know anything about this guy."

"I do," Jayne said, raising a hand. "He's rumored to be an excellent lover."

"You guys!" Eden rolled her eyes. "You're putting the cart way before the horse."

"And you're just scared to take a chance." Ashley made clucking noises and flapped her arms like a chicken. "Admit it."

"Okay, guilty as charged. I'm scared spitless."

"What are you afraid of?" Jayne asked.

"Oh, no," Ashley teased, dramatically clutching her head in her hands and moaning. "Now you've gone and done it."

"Done what?" Jayne glanced from Ashley to Eden.

"You've given an 'in' to her worst-case scenario voice."

"Her what?"

Eden glared at Ashley. "Thanks a lot."

"Go ahead," Ashley said. "Show Jayne how neurotic you can get."

"It's not neurotic to project future complications based on current information." Eden pursed out her bottom lip. "It's merely prudent."

"Let's do it then," Ashley challenged her.

"All right," she said, deciding to play the game her impertinent assistant had invented in defense against Eden's worrywart tendency. She had to confess, the game often worked to quell her fears when little else did. She squared off with Ashley toe-to-toe. "What if he has bad breath?"

"Then give him a Tic-Tac."

"What if he's a rotten kisser?"

"You explain to him exactly how you prefer to be kissed."

"What if he has an itty-bitty penis?"

"It's the motion of the ocean that counts, all that matters is that he rocks your boat."

Jayne giggled. "You two are so funny."

"Okay," Eden said, growing serious as she risked expressing the real fears pyramiding inside her. "What if he thinks *I'm* a lousy lay?"

"Ooh," Jayne said. "I can help you with that one. If there's ever anything you want to know about driving a man wild in bed, I'm your go-to gal. Call me anytime."

Ashley spread her palms. "There you are. Problems solved."

Eden gulped. "All right, smarty-pants. Here's the biggie. Worst-case scenario. What if he's repulsed by my burn scars, can't get it up when he sees me naked and then he rejects me?"

Undaunted, Ashley jutted out her chin and challenged, "Best-case scenario. He thinks you're beautiful no matter your scars and your crazy worst-case-scenario voice. He's a great kisser with minty breath and he's got a gigantic penis. You have splendid sex and get your creativity back. Business booms, you fall madly in love, get married, buy a house in Connecticut, have three kids, two cats and a Pomeranian named Kibble and thirty years from now you're still playing Tarzan and Jane with each other just like Mr. and Mrs. Lockerbee."

Eden sucked in her breath. Did she dare to dream

that dream? Was she brave enough to take a step toward claiming her sexuality?

Do it. Take a chance. What have you got to lose?

What indeed?

She'd been holding herself in reserve for too long. By not taking risks, she'd closed herself off to her creative wellspring. She needed more intimacy, not only with her work, but with her body as well.

She glanced at the basket in the window, the one completely lacking in pizzazz. That unexciting basket made her decision for her. If she wanted to get her inspiration back she had to take charge and move forcefully toward her goals.

She was going to lunch with Alec Ramsey. How else would she ever discover if those sparks between them would come to nothing or might lead to something wickedly wonderful?

3
_____

THE NEXT MORNING excitement over his upcoming date with Eden had Alec prowling the hallways of the *Single Guy* offices located on the fourteenth floor of Trump Towers. His exuberant edginess, as it so often did, spilled over onto his employees.

He was walking fast and talking faster, okaying cover art for the upcoming edition, sending a writer back to the drawing board on a feature article that hadn't turned out as expected, double-checking appointments with his executive assistant, Holden.

Everyone took his or her cue from his go-go-go attitude. They were keyed up and working at a frantic pace. Everyone, that is, except taciturn Holden, who always remained calm no matter what was happening around him. The young man's unruffled aplomb was the very reason Alec had hired him. He needed an assistant who balanced his own impulsive nature. Holden kept him grounded when Alec might have otherwise gotten off track following his quicksilver mind wherever it chose to flow.

"Reschedule my one-o'clock workout with Randy," Alec told Holden. "Something's come up."

Holden, who at twenty-two was more efficient than

many executive assistants twice his age, swiftly made a notation in his Palm Pilot. "Oh, and by the way, your uncle is in your office."

"Mac?" Alec broke into a smile. "He's back from Fiji?"

Holden nodded. "Helping himself to your Scotch, I might add."

"He can help himself to anything he wants," Alec's grin widened. "I am what I am today because of Uncle Mac."

"I'll restock."

Alec pushed into his office to find his tanned, lean-muscled uncle sitting cocked back in the plush leather chair that had once belonged to him. Mac looked a little tired, however, that is until he flashed Alec a row of straight white teeth and raised his tumbler of Scotch in a salute.

"You old dog!" Alec exclaimed, slipping around the desk to embrace Mac in a bear hug as he rose to his feet. "You're back early."

"There's only so much of those warm tropical breezes and sultry island girls a man can take."

"Yeah, right."

Mac set his glass down and feigned a boxing move. Alec feigned in return. They embraced again, slapping each other on the back. His father's younger brother had never been married and never aspired to be. He was the consummate playboy and Alec's mentor, teaching him everything he knew both about the publishing industry and how to seduce women. For forty-nine years Mac had lived the very life he extolled in the pages of *Single Guy* before turning over the helm to Alec and Randy the previous year.

"So," Mac prompted. "Any interesting conquests while I was gone?"

"Nope, no one." Alec shook his head. Without understanding why, he really didn't want to tell Mac about Eden. Besides, there wasn't much to tell.

Yet.

Mac wagged his head. "Boy, you'll never live up to my reputation if you keep spending so much time on the sidelines."

"You're a legend, Uncle Mac, there's no living up to you."

His uncle laughed, but the jocularity seemed forced and Alec wondered if something was wrong. "Well, you might not be the hound dog I was, but you've got the soft soap down pat."

"Thanks, I guess."

"By the way." Mac tapped the October issue of *Single Guy* lying open on the desk. "While I was waiting on you I checked out your last editorial. All Women Are Goddesses, Let's Treat Them That Way." He hooted. "You really believe that?"

"Yes. Don't you?" Alec *did* believe women were goddesses. Nothing fascinated him more than the fairer sex. He loved the smell of them, their softness, the way their minds worked. Chalk it up to having four sisters. Fact was, he adored the women. Tall ones, short ones, plump ones, thin ones. He made no discrimination. That's why he couldn't commit to just one. There were simply too many wonderful ladies walking the face of the earth.

"*All* women are goddesses?" Mac arched an eyebrow.

"All women," Alec said firmly.

"Even the…"

"Don't go there." Alec shook his head.

"Your Eagle Scout ethics are showing, but I'm betting that article got you laid ten times over."

"Actually no. That's part of the new sexual etiquette. No taking advantage of provocative situations."

"Hell, then what's the point? You might as well get married along with your buddy Randy."

Alec studied his uncle. Something was going on. "You know I'm not interested in getting married."

"Just remember that. The last thing you want is to end up straitjacketed in suburbia, working two jobs to support five kids, only to die of a heart attack way before your time."

"That wouldn't happen to me."

"Because I made it my mission in life to save you from my brother's fate. Thank God, I succeeded. Can you imagine yourself living in Connecticut and trotting home on the train to your sweet little wife who'll only give you nooky twice a month with the lights off if you're lucky, three rug-rats with attention deficit disorder, two neurotic cats and a dog who won't quit peeing on the carpet?"

"No, I can't imagine it." Alec shifted his weight uncomfortably.

They'd had this conversation many times before and, while he was glad to see Mac, he really didn't want to get his uncle started on his favorite soapbox issue.

What he wanted was to get on the phone and make reservations for his lunch with Eden. He could have gotten Holden to make the arrangements, but for some odd reason Alec wanted to handle it himself. He glanced at his wristwatch.

"I won't keep you," Mac said, picking up on his signal. "I just dropped by to invite you to dinner with Sophie and me."

"Which one is she again?"

"You remember Sophie. I've dated her on and off for fifteen years. Leggy redhead, Southern accent, killer rack."

"Now, now," Alec chided. He'd never realized before how immature his uncle sometimes sounded. "No objectifying women."

Mac shook his head. "Good thing I retired when I did. I can't keep up with all these new rules. Oh, by the way, Sophie's got a date all lined up for you."

Alec winced. "Listen, Mac, I don't know about this blind date."

"Shh. You're the publisher of *Single Guy.* You've got a reputation to uphold and, seeing as how your partner has decided to up and get married, the mantle of sustained bachelorhood rests firmly on your shoulders. Gotta show the world you're all about the fun. Besides, Sophie says her friend used to be a circus acrobat.'' Mac winked. ''Bet you never dated one of those.''

''You got me there.''

''I'll send a car around at six. We're going to see *The Producers* after dinner at Kim Sum's. I'll spring for the check.''

Alec didn't want to go on a blind date, but he hadn't seen Mac for over a month. It was the least he could do for his uncle. ''Sure. Okay. See you tonight.''

The minute the door closed behind Mac, Alec plopped into his chair and reached for the telephone. Circus acrobat be damned. He had a sexy, erotic gift-basket designer on the hook and he wasn't about to let her get away.

Alec made reservations at an intimate restaurant on Forty-fourth Street that was way overpriced for lunch, but what the hell? What was the point of having money if you couldn't use it to spoil a special lady? He was definitely looking to impress her.

Eden represented the kind of naughty, no-strings-attached relationship he'd been searching for since Randy had announced his engagement. Showing her a great time would remind him exactly how good it was to be single, footloose and fancy-free.

He rubbed his palms together, requested the restaurant's most expensive bottle of champagne, asked them to ice it and then called his florist to order a small bouquet of flowers. He planned on laying his cards on the table, giving Eden the full court press. He wanted her to know exactly what was on his mind—that he was very attracted to her, but he wasn't the marrying kind.

Alec didn't want to waste either of their time with silly mind games, nor did he want her to get hurt. If his initial impression of her had been wrong and she wasn't all about fun and adventure, then he needed to know that now.

Because ever since their electric meeting yesterday afternoon, Alec had only one goal on his mind.

Seducing Eden Montgomery.

"YOU WERE RIGHT," Jayne Lockerbee told Sarah Ramsey Armstrong. "They are perfect for each other. Sparks flew the minute they laid eyes on each other."

Sarah pushed a strand of sleek blond hair behind one multipierced ear and grinned over the top of her cubicle at her co-worker. They were both financial analysts for Dean-Sterns Investments, although Jayne worked only three days a week.

"When you gave Zach and me that erotic gift basket for a wedding present I knew whoever had made it was exactly the kind of woman Alec needed. Earthy, grounded, intelligent and yet incredibly sensual."

"That's Eden to a tee—even if she doesn't yet have the self-confidence to realize her feminine power. But with our help, she will." Jayne grinned.

"Yes! Enough with the airheaded bimbos already. Alec goes for them because they're not a threat. My brother needs someone who'll challenge him both inside the bedroom and out, whether he knows it or not.'' Sarah clapped. ''Making this match is going to be such fun.''

''Are you sure Alec is ready to settle down?'' Jayne frowned. ''I care about Eden and I don't want to see her hurt. She's vulnerable, especially since the fire. I think the last guy she was seeing really did a number on her ego.''

''Relax. My little brother's got his faults, but he's not a heartbreaker.''

''But he publishes a magazine worshiping the merits of bachelorhood over marriage and he has dated a lot of women,'' Jayne mused.

Sarah waved a dismissive hand. ''A lot of what you see is public relations. Alec doesn't treat women frivolously and he hasn't had nearly as many girlfriends as he likes everyone to believe.''

''Really?''

''Now, he wouldn't admit it if you tortured him, but I've seen the wistful way he looks at Randy and Jill and me and Zach. No matter how much he protests to the contrary, he's not built like Uncle Mac. Sooner or later he's going to realize what he's missing by clinging to his silly belief that love and marriage mean the death of fun and freedom. And I think your Eden is just the woman to teach him how to face his fears. He's going to love the intimacy of monogamy once he gets a taste of it.''

''How do you know?''

Sarah held out her left hand and admired the big diamond sparkling there. ''Until I met Zach, I was afraid of commitment, too. We Ramseys are a stubborn bunch, but when we do fall in love, we're in it for the long haul.''

''I remember.'' Jayne laughed. ''I kept trying to tell you what a wonderful thing a good marriage was.''

''So I'm a slow learner. Let's hope Alec realizes sooner than I did that there's nothing more profound than finding your soul mate. Not to mention hot, hot, hot.''

''The sexual chemistry between those two *was* unmistakable,'' Jayne said. ''I thought Eden's boutique was going to combust.''

''All they needed was a push in the right direction.'' Sarah nodded. ''They'll thank us in the end.''

''I'll call Eden after she comes back from their luncheon and see how things went.''

''I'll keep you posted on what Alec says.''

The two women grinned at each other and Sarah started humming the matchmaker song from *Fiddler on the Roof.*

WOULD LIGHTNING STRIKE twice? Or had yesterday simply been a fluke?

Wetting her lips to dampen her nervousness, Eden changed from her Nikes in the ground-floor ladies' room at Trump Towers and slipped into the pair of four-inch Jimmy Choo ebony sling-backs Jayne had loaned her.

Was Alec Ramsey really the man she wanted as her love mentor?

That was the question she was here to answer.

In the meantime, she had caved in to Ashley and Jayne's demands that she vamp out, although she couldn't shake the feeling she was leading Alec on, acting like an experienced, sexually confident woman when that's the last thing she was.

"Act the part," Ashley had encouraged when she'd insisted Eden borrow her skintight black leather skirt that was long enough to hide Eden's burn scars but short enough to generate plenty of head-turning interest. On the subway ride over she'd gotten a half-dozen appreciative wolf whistles.

"Perceiving, behaving, becoming," Jayne had imparted along with the Jimmy Choos, and a pair of dynamite black fishnet stockings with sparkly rhinestones sewn into the back seam.

But what had finally convinced her to give their plan a try was the editorial in the front pages of the October issue of *Single Guy*. She was impressed by the way Alec advocated responsible sex and described all woman as goddesses. As the publisher of a magazine aimed at bachelors, he might be commitment shy, but reading the article clued her in that Alec definitely knew how to indulge a lady.

And that was exactly what she needed. A temporary tryst with a tender and considerate man who wouldn't head for the hills when he discovered her secret.

Eden peered at herself in the bathroom mirror and was startled to see how unruly she appeared. She ran a hand through her rowdy curls to tame them. The humid weather played havoc with her hair, giving her a just-tumbled-out-of-bed look. Her lipstick color too red, her mascara too thickly applied.

Bad-girl glam.

She felt restless and reckless and edgy. And those alien feelings scared her. She wished she'd had the courage to explore her sexuality more fully before the fire, before she had the scars to contend with, but she'd been too chicken. Frightened of catching a communicable disease or of ending up like her mother or of getting her heart broken.

Or all three.

Which was why she was in the situation she was in now. Sexually frustrated, with her creativity stagnant. Dared she hope that Alec Ramsey held the key to her liberation?

She glanced at her watch. Five minutes to one.

"Show time," she whispered to her reflection, slipped her sneakers into her satchel, took a deep breath and headed for the fourteenth floor.

Controlled chaos greeted her when she stepped off the elevator and pushed through the double glass doors with *Single Guy* etched into the panels with a bold, masculine font.

Phones rang incessantly. People hurried to and fro squeezing past each other in the narrow corridor at the same time someone was holding an impromptu sales meeting right there at the central credenza.

The walls were bright and splashy, featuring advertisers' posters hawking everything from imported liquor to expensive automobiles to the trendiest menswear fashions.

Copies of *Single Guy* were stacked everywhere. Executive toys rested on computers and desktops. Daring alternative rock music blared from a high-tech sound system and a help-yourself popcorn machine filled the air with the scent of freshly popped, buttered popcorn.

The place was energetic, lively and imaginative. A grown-up guy's playground. And Alec was right in the big middle of the free-for-all.

Eden stood to one side for a moment, watching him.

He wore a black turtleneck sweater and formfitting trousers that showed off his breathtaking physique. His longish hair was sexily tousled. His profile was dazzling—regal nose, rugged chin, high cheekbones.

Her pulse bounded through her veins at a feverish pace as the *William Tell Overture* galloped crazily inside her head.

He migrated from person to person, pumping his employees up, urging them to give a hundred and ten percent to the job at hand. He brainstormed concepts on the fly, storytelling, networking and motivating with nothing more than a smile and his irresistible presence.

She quickly realized he managed his team with the mental equivalent of chain-saw juggling. He kept a permanent smile hardwired to his chiseled features. He was everything she was not. Witty, inspirational, charming, impulsive.

Without a doubt this mover and shaker would be a dynamo between the sheets. If she slept with him, would some of that high-energy enthusiasm rub off on her? She hoped so.

Eden noticed a serious-looking young man hovering at Alec's elbow. He was keeping up with everything that transpired, calmly and methodically jotting down notes in a Palm Pilot.

Ah, she thought, the follow-through guy. Alec was the idea man; the younger dude was the one who made it all come together. Alec was smart enough to surround himself with the right people.

In that brief span of two minutes, Eden's admiration for him doubled. Oh, to be so spontaneous, so unselfconscious, so alive.

Alec pivoted on his heel, spun in Eden's direction and stopped cold.

The minute he spotted her, his grin widened and his eyes rounded. He looked as if he's just won an Atlantic City jackpot. The million-dollar expression in his eyes went a long way in repairing her damaged self-esteem and earning him a hundred brownie points toward becoming the lover she finally let see her scar.

''Wow,'' he said, low and husky as he stalked closer, ''look at you.''

Leisurely, he combed his gaze from the top of her head, down her low-cut red sweater, to the snug-fitting leather skirt, to her fishnet stockings, to the sexy stilettos and back again. Her clothes issued a provocative message Eden feared she could not back up. A long moment passed and she almost turned and ran.

But the appreciative look in Alec's eyes held her anchored to the spot.

The entire office had followed his movements and now all of his employees were staring at her, obviously intrigued by the woman who'd captured their dynamic boss's interest.

Eden felt her cheeks flush. Oh great. She was blushing like a schoolgirl. But no man this influential had ever had quite this reaction to her before. She had longed for this very outcome when she'd donned her sexy outfit, but now that she had his undivided attention, she wasn't sure what to do with it.

She smiled shyly and raised a hand to her throat. "I overdressed, didn't I?"

"No. Oh, no. You look absolutely gorgeous. Are you ready to get down to business?" His gray eyes smoldered with a sexuality that took her breath away and his full, masculine lips held her mesmerized.

"Pardon?" Eden blinked. She'd been fantasizing about kissing him and his question caught her off guard.

"Lunch, the gift consultation."

"Oh, yes." She patted her satchel. "I've got everything right here."

"Yes, you do." He grinned rakishly, allowed his eyes to take another trip over her body and Eden knew he wasn't talking about what was in her portfolio.

In that moment, she made her decision. In spite of the nervousness knotting her stomach, in spite of her fears that he was anticipating a femme fatale and there was no way she could measure up to his expectations, in spite of the gamble she was taking by risking his ultimate rejection, Eden knew what she wanted.

Correction, what she desperately needed in order to recover her creative self-confidence.

A red-hot fling with the sumptuous Alec Ramsey.

4

ALEC TOOK HER to Maison Henri, an elegant new French restaurant in Midtown. He opened the door for her, lightly grasped her elbow and guided her in over the threshold.

Eden appreciated his proprietary touch. It made her feel protected. Her pulse accelerated at the casual contact and immediately a half-dozen sexual fantasies tumbled through her mind exactly as they had the day before. The same fantasies that had vanished the minute he'd left her shop.

The more she was around him, the more she suspected this man was indeed her sexual muse. A decidedly masculine version of the mythical Erato. Eden shivered at the fanciful notion.

Careful, Eden.

Starry-eyed romanticism had led her into that disastrous relationship with Josh. She had to be careful. Her fragile ego couldn't handle another mistake like that one.

The maître d' greeted them and led them to their table tucked behind a wooden partition draped with artificial grape vines. He pulled out her chair for her and then, with a flourish, settled a white linen napkin in her lap.

"Thank you," Eden murmured, and glanced over at Alec.

His eyes were on her face. "This place is a little extravagant, but I thought perhaps you might enjoy something special."

"It was very thoughtful of you."

Eden felt like a powerful politician's mistress meeting her lover for a clandestine tryst in the dimly lighted, quaint bistro at one-thirty in the afternoon. Only three other couples were in the restaurant and they were seated at the far end of the room. The isolated privacy, the decadent aroma of mouthwateringly rich food scenting the air and the flickering candlelight heightened the romantic mood.

Their garçon, efficient and ghostlike, waited at the ready with two menus and a wine list in his hand. A bottle of shockingly expensive champagne sat chilling in a bucket beside Alec's elbow.

A nosegay of pansies graced the center of the table. Eden loved the delicate, colorful flowers and was surprised to see the card propped against the small bouquet with her name on it.

Oh, my.

"The flowers are for me?"

"Go ahead, read the card."

Tentatively she reached for the envelope and opened it with shaky fingers.

From one sensualist to another, Alec.

Uh-oh. Because of her unusual profession, Alec

had assumed she was much more sexually knowl-
edgeable than she actually was. She hoped he wasn't
disappointed when he learned the truth about her.

If he learned the truth, she reminded herself. Keep
things low-key for the time being. Feel out the situation before proceeding. Pretend this is nothing more
than a business luncheon.

"The flowers are beautiful," she said, feeling
bowled over by his attentions, and dropped the card
into her purse. "Thank you." The garçon handed
them their menus and an awkward silence ensued as
they studied the choices.

"The coq au vin here is excellent," Alec said.

"I'll have that then." She smiled and passed the
menu back to the garçon. "And a house salad with
vinaigrette dressing."

"Oui, mademoiselle. Et pour vous, monsieur?"

"I'll have the same," Alec replied.

The garçon bowed and left.

"It's too formal here." Alec made a regretful face.
"I went over the top."

"No, no, it's fine," she reassured him. "Very elegant."

"I gravitate toward grand gestures. My sisters say
it's because I'm a show-off."

In that moment he seemed as vulnerable as a little
boy gifting his mother with a dandelion bouquet and
holding his breath waiting for her approval.

Why, he's just as nervous as I am. She was touched
that he cared enough to be anxious and the realization
relaxed her a little.

"I'm flattered you consider me worthy of a grand gesture," Eden admitted, while at the same time worrying that things were moving too quickly. "This is a great place."

"Really?"

"It's lovely."

He looked relieved and grateful for her kind words. He wasn't nearly as cool and suave as she'd first supposed and she found his humanity endearing.

"Why don't we get down to business while we're waiting for our food." She lowered her voice and glanced over her shoulder to make sure the waiter wasn't still hovering. "Let's discuss your friends' secret sexual fantasies."

"Excuse me?" He blinked at her as if he'd been caught napping.

"Randy and Jill. Their wedding present. The reason we're here."

"Oh, yeah, that."

"Generally, I start the process with a basic fantasy. For instance the fantasy inspiration for your sister Sarah's Palm Tree Passion basket was Island Girl and Surfer Dude."

"I'm not sure I want to hear about my sister's sexual fantasies. Thank you very much."

Eden chuckled. "Okay, I see what you mean. That was just an example."

She took the portfolio from her satchel and opened it up to reveal pictures of gift baskets she had created. She scooted her chair closer to his side of the table so they could both see the book.

The warmth of his breath feathered the hairs along the nape of her neck as he leaned in closer. She turned her head to look at him. Lowering her lashes, she shyly issued him a provocative invitation with her eyes. Worst-case scenarios aside, this was turning out to be much easier than she expected.

"Tell me if anything strikes a chord with you."

"Will do."

It was a strange sensation, Alec watching her so intently. She found she couldn't quite lose herself in the moment. His smoky-gray eyes split her focus between the portfolio and her awareness of him studying her.

He made her feel beautiful, she realized, and *that* unnerved her too. She wasn't accustomed to captivating a man's attention so completely. Especially a man as handsome and dynamic as this one. That feeling dared her to act bolder, more confidently, urging her to be everything that he saw in her.

"What's this one called?" Alec tapped the first photograph.

"Here we have the Professor and the Vixen. That basket might include things like reading glasses, feather boas, classical music tapes, or even a whip."

The sleeve of his shirt lightly grazed her forearm and damn if a shower of sparks didn't shoot through her body. Eden blew out her breath slowly to diffuse the stunning heat.

He shook his head. "I don't think so."

"The Rock Star and the Groupie?"

"Nah."

Eden flipped the page. "Master and Slave?"

Alec wriggled his eyebrows at her.

"You think they'd like that one?"

"No, but I would."

She felt her cheeks start to burn, but then she denied the blush and fought it off. She was a professional. She did this for a living. She refused to be ashamed or embarrassed by frank sexual talk.

"Which do you fancy," she teased, slanting him a sidelong glance. "Role-playing the master or the slave?"

"Oh," he said, "I'm totally democratic. I believe in taking turns."

"I'll have to keep that in mind." Oh my gosh, had she just said that? Eden longed to slap her hand over her mouth, but she didn't.

His gray eyes crinkled at the corners. "What else you got?"

"Tie Me Up, Tie Me Down?"

"Another intriguing prospect."

In her mind's eye she vividly saw Alec laying buck naked tied to a poster bed in four-point restraints and instant moisture dampened her panties. Her body ached all over with sudden need. How was it possible that a virtual stranger made her feel so recklessly intense? She swallowed hard and struggled to appear composed.

"More." He waved a hand.

Eden shook her head to dispel the visual images that didn't want to leave. "The Biker and Lady Godiva. We're talking leather and chains, long blond wig for Lady Godiva, that sort of thing.''

"Good one, but let's keep looking."

"The Chauffeur and the Countessa?"

"Perhaps."

"The Playboy and the Virgin?"

Alec snapped his fingers. "There. Now that sounds perfect for Randy and Jill. What sort of items do you see in that one?"

Eden sucked in her breath. He had chosen *her* favorite fantasy. The uninitiated virgin's sexual awakening at the hands of a master seducer thrilled Eden to her core. Her mind, which for the past few weeks had been completely sluggish when it came to new and sexy ideas, filled with a hundred intriguing possibilities.

"W-well," she stuttered, and wondered why she was stammering. "In my creations I appeal to all five senses. We start with the crucible. The basket is not always an actual basket, you know. It can be anything from a motorcycle helmet to a briefcase to an Igloo cooler."

"Ah. So in the case of The Playboy and the Virgin, we might use a champagne bucket instead of a basket."

"Exactly. Let me make some notes." She started to reach for her satchel again, but he pulled a pen from his coat pocket and held it out to her.

"Oh, thank you." Tentatively she reached out.

Her fingertips brushed his and she nearly came unraveled. She took the pen, still warm from his body heat. The longer she held it, the warmer it grew against her skin. She gulped.

Excitement, along with a good deal of fear, sizzled through her veins. Hurriedly she scribbled on a yellow legal pad that she kept tucked in her portfolio and didn't dare look up.

"Okay," she said, after she'd jotted down what they had so far and passed that volatile pen back to him. How a simple writing instrument could evoke such tumultuous emotions in her she had no idea, but she couldn't get rid of the pen fast enough. "I usually line the baskets with something. It can simply be a piece of fabric, or it can be a garment. Like a negligee or scarf. I've got fabric swatches."

She flipped to the back of the portfolio, where she had glued small squares of sensual fabrics, and held her breath. Did she have the courage to continue the sensual exercise she performed with a client when helping them pick out the right cloth?

What if the erotic little exercise turned into a best-case scenario and led back to his apartment for some afternoon delight as Ashley so succinctly put it? What if she got what she wanted only to discover too late she wasn't the kind of woman who could separate love and great sex?

Eden hesitated a long moment.

Go on. It's your job. Just do it.

"Have fabric swatches, will design?" he quipped, gave her a friendly wink and a lopsided grin.

Whatever happened, whichever way it went down, at least she'd have fun with this guy. Besides, there was only one way to break out of her rut—plunge ahead. Bolstering her courage, Eden made her move.

"Close your eyes," she whispered.

"Hmm," Alec closed his eyes. "I like the sounds of this."

"Give me your hand."

Obediently he held out his hand and almost groaned aloud when her skin seared his. The pure charge of electrical passion that raged up his arm turned his world topsy-turvy.

She used his fingers to trace the material. The soft brush of velvet sent a bolt of desire blasting through his hard body.

"Velvet," he murmured.

"Now," she whispered. "Imagine your naked skin immersed in these materials."

Dear God, did the woman have even a remote idea what she was doing to him?

She guided his fingertips over lithe silk, smooth satin, plush mink, glossy taffeta, nubby corduroy, scratchy tweed. She sauntered his fingers on a trip around the world with luxurious chenille, stiff Irish lace and sumptuous angora. Together they stroked rich cashmere and supple suede and stonewashed denim.

And with each touch, each journey, easy smooth glide, he grew more and more aroused. He would feel the imprint of her hand on his for days. He had to bite down on his tongue to keep from groaning.

He was dying to open his eyes and gaze into her face. He wanted to see if she'd been as deeply affected by their connection as he. He wanted more. To see more of her, touch more, feel more. He wanted to rip off her clothes and ravish her right here on the restaurant table while he licked and sucked and tasted every inch of her. What would you call that fantasy? The Caveman and the Epicurean?

"So which material do you think they will like best?" she murmured.

"Who?" he asked, opening his eyes and blinking away the dazed fog of sexual fantasies clogging his brain. Thank heavens Eden had no idea what he'd just been thinking.

"Randy and Jill."

Oh yeah, them. "Too many choices," he said.

"Focus on our theme. The Playboy and the Virgin."

"If the champagne bucket represents the playboy, the liner should represent the virgin."

"Exactly. We need something soft and pure and delicate."

"Angora," they said in unison.

"Hey." Eden laughed. "You're pretty good at this."

"Line the champagne bucket with an angora sweater. Jill's favorite color is blue and she wears a size six," he said.

"Next," Eden said, as she chuckled huskily and flipped the page, "come the sex toys."

Lordy. The page was filled with every erotic gadget known to man. And Alec had thought he was stiff before, as he imagined a dozen different ways of trying out those gadgets on Eden.

"I was thinking a chastity belt." She tapped a picture of the sex toy version of a chastity belt complete with a red heart-shaped lock and matching skeleton key.

"If Jill wears that, Randy will be steamed up in nothing flat."

"That's the idea."

"He's a man who can't resist a challenge."

"Just like his best friend, huh?"

There she was again, reading him like an open book. It was an unsettling talent. He took a sip of water to cool himself off.

"And as for the playboy," she said. "We'll need a very sophisticated play toy." When she pointed to one, Alec just about choked on his water.

"You okay?" she asked.

"Uh-huh" was all he could manage, and he waved a hand for her to continue.

"I could even write out a script for their playacting if you think that's something they would enjoy," Eden said. "Some customers appreciate having scripts to get their creative juices flowing."

Babe, you've already got my juices flowing.

"Could you give me an example?" He knew he was naughty for making her describe the script in detail, but he couldn't help himself. One glance into those scintillating blue eyes and he ached to be a very bad boy indeed.

Would she take the bait? Alec focused on her

small, full mouth as she slowly slipped out the tip of her sweet, pink tongue and ran it over her lips.

"Okay," she said. "This erotic scenario takes place on the playboy's territory. Somewhere urbane. His penthouse apartment perhaps."

Alec thought of his own penthouse apartment and gulped.

"Or maybe a hotel in Paris with a view of the Champs Elysee."

"Uh-huh."

"The lighting is just right. The music is smooth and sexy." Her face took on a dreamy expression as if she herself were in that Paris hotel room. "The virgin is oh, so scared but she wants this so badly. Her knees tremble, her pulse pounds, her body heats up as he hands her a glass of champagne and speaks to her in the language of love."

Eden murmured something very naughty in French and his animal instincts roared through his body. It was all Alec could do to keep from pulling her into his lap and kissing her right then and there.

Seemingly unaware of the physical turmoil she'd generated in him, Eden moved a palm in imitation of a panning camera. "The windows are open. The breeze blows her sheer nightgown against her bare legs. The playboy comes closer, a rakish gleam in his eyes. The inexperienced innocent wants him to teach her everything he knows."

Eden stopped.

"Go on."

She glanced nervously over her shoulder. "We're in a public place."

"And out of earshot of anyone."

She softened her voice so he could barely hear her. "In painstaking detail the playboy tells her exactly what he's going to do to her before it happens. How he's going to undress her. How he's going to run his hot hands over her silken body. How he's going to suck her nipples until they are hard pebbles in his mouth."

The hairs on the back of his neck raised and so did something far south of his neck. He was going to have to stop her from continuing or embarrass himself.

"Yeah," Alec said hoarsely. "A script sounds good. Go with that."

"Will do."

Alec realized he had a death grip on the arms of his chair and forced himself to unhinge his fingers. With her head ducked, Eden's lush chestnut hair fell tantalizingly forward, giving him just a peek of her profile.

She smelled of baby powder. Sweet and talcy. The scent surprised him. He had expected her to smell of exotic perfume or of the spicy cinnamon aroma that permeated her boutique.

The pleasantly chalky scent blindsided him. Baby powder and erotic gift basket designer didn't jibe. She should smell like bold primary colors not delicate pastels. The foxy outfit she wore screamed *look at me* but her fragrance whispered *treat-me-tender*.

Baby powder suggested innocence, naivete, a certain simplicity that was exactly opposite of the image she projected. The smell made him think of babies and bath time and lullabies.

Babies made him think of mothers. And mothers made him think of wives. And wives made him think of marriage. And marriage made him think of boredom and restriction and getting old.

A flit of memory flashed through his brain. He remembered one of the rare times his father had been home between his two full-time jobs and Alec had run to him with his baseball and catcher's mitt. "Come on, Dad. Let's play," he'd begged. His father, looking weary and worn, had shaken his head. "Can't, son. Somebody's gotta mow the lawn."

The bite of sadness at that small slice of recall still stung. But later that same afternoon, after his father had mowed the lawn and gone inside to take a nap, Uncle Mac had zoomed into the driveway in his Corvette, flashed two tickets to the Yankees game and Alec's day had been transformed.

Alec shook off the memory.

Dammit. Having an affair with Eden was supposed to make him forget about mundane things like marriage and kids and death and taxes. She was supposed to remind him how great it was to be single, how lucky he was not to have a ring on his finger or the smell of baby powder in his life.

The paradox inherent within Eden kicked him with a swift reality check. Was he sure he really wanted to get involved with her if she made him think about the very things he desperately wanted to ignore?

And then, before he could debate the question further, she raised her gaze and gave him a smile so brash and naughty, all doubts flew from his mind.

Alec studied her; the inquisitive tilt to her head, her delicate ears studded with pearls, her soft blue eyes clouded with sexual desire, her small but perfectly shaped lips, full and luxuriously painted in opulent crimson.

He wanted her. With a hunger so fierce it scared him. No woman had ever so completely held his imagination hostage.

Driven on by a relentless sexual impulse he could not deny, he made his move before he'd fully thought this thing through.

He reached out, laid his hand on her upper thigh and whispered, "I want you."

EDEN JUMPED from her chair so quickly it overturned and hit the floor with a resounding thud. Thank heavens for the vine-covered partition blocking them from the other diners.

Her thigh, just below where her scars lurked, smoldered from his touch. An inch higher and he would have felt the irregular lines and ultratender skin of her disfigurement.

Her heart hammered, her stomach roller-coastered and her knees bumped together.

Alec reached down and righted her chair. The garçon hurried over to see if anything was wrong, but Alec waved him away.

"I'm sorry," he said as she sat back down. "I was

out of line touching you like that. Obviously, I misread the signals.''

Eden tried to think of the right thing to say, to extricate herself from the situation without hurting his feelings or alienating him to the point of ruining any chance for an affair. She *had* led him on. Except when things turned heavy-duty and he'd got too close, she'd panicked and jerked away.

Because of the scars.

"You didn't do anything wrong, Alec. You just startled me. I was expecting...I didn't know..."

"I moved too fast."

"Yes. No. I just wasn't ready."

"The fault is entirely mine." He shoved his fingers through his hair. "I've got to learn to stop being so impulsive. I feel something, I act on it. It often gets me into trouble."

"But impulsiveness isn't always a bad thing."

"It is if it chases you away."

He looked so distraught, Eden knew she had to do something to make him feel better. Without another word, she leaned over and right there in the middle of the restaurant, like the bold, sexually assertive woman he believed her to be, and filched a kiss.

Alec's eyes widened in shocked surprise.

She had never done anything so spontaneous, so out of character, so unpredictable, and she loved it. For the first time in her life, she understood what it felt like to simply let loose and let go and allow nature to take its course.

Amazing.

And it didn't take Alec long to recover. He quickly took command, overpowering her warm, willing mouth with his own. He branded her with his wayward tongue, seared her with his tempting passion.

Her heart did a free fall, tripping at a frantic rhythm of stimulus and response. She sighed against his lips as he used his tongue to coax her into a teasing game of thrust and parry.

He sucked softly at her bottom lip, pulling it in and out of his mouth in a smooth sucking maneuver. He'd recovered pretty quickly from her surprise attack. In fact, it was Eden's turn to feel confused as his tongue muddled her brain.

Briefly he pulled away and said, "I've spent the last twenty-four hours wondering what you taste like."

"Did I live up to your expectations?"

"Babe, you surpassed 'em," he murmured, and went back to kissing her.

She could say the same for him. He tasted of cool, saucy peppermint and hot, delicious sin.

Eden closed her eyes and inhaled him, exploring his taste layer by layer. There was the peppermint, refreshing and icily warm. He tasted lively and curious. His flavor was all stylish attitude—suave and debonair. One hundred percent dashing playboy.

The man knew exactly what he was doing. The kiss and his taste took her higher, hotter, transporting her into the realm of memory and fantasy.

He tasted like Christmas, like snowmen, like her grandfather's favorite English mints. He tasted like fun and freedom and frivolity. His taste made her at once giddy and dizzy and oh, so happy to be alive.

He kissed with a power and authority born of long practice and she realized she was jealous of that rehearsal. She was jealous of all the women who'd gotten to kiss him. And of all the things she'd been missing simply because she'd been too afraid to step outside her comfort zone.

His lips sang with chaos and energy and challenging charm. His kiss whispered of the unimagined delights that awaited her if she would just take that last step toward laying down her guard.

She'd picked herself a winner.

And she wished the kissing would go on and on and on forever.

In Alec's arms she felt as if she could accomplish anything.

Creative block? What creative block?

A thousand imaginative ideas exploded in her brain, each and everyone involving Alec and the Kama Sutra and sex toys and erotic scripts and role-playing and using food inappropriately and...

"Pardon," the garçon said, clearing his throat and shattering their fantasy world. "Your coq au vin."

5

THE POWER OF HER KISS overwhelmed him.

She'd seized him by surprise. Surprise, hell. Her ambush was the mental equivalent of catching him with his pants down. He was shocked and amazed and mightily impressed. If they gave Olympic medals for kissing, Eden Montgomery would take home the gold.

By crook or by hook, he had to have her.

He waited just long enough for the garçon to vamoose before he looked across the table at her. Her fetching blue eyes met his with a sheen of appetite that had nothing to do with the gourmet meal in front of them.

They fell into each other's gazes. He stared hard, communicating his want with his expression. She met his challenge, didn't blink. She peered into his eyes as if she knew all his secrets, all his flaws, all his mistakes and she liked him anyway.

God, but she was one helluva woman. Vibrant. Adventuresome. And not the least bit afraid of her sexuality.

She was exactly what he'd been searching for.

Her attractiveness went much deeper than surface

appeal. Sure, she was pretty, but her looks weren't what captivated him. Rather it was her zest, her fire, her lusty attitude that snatched him by the short hairs and refused to let go. Her sensuality was intrinsic, interlaced within her flesh and bones, not blatant or fabricated or unnatural.

She was earthy and alert and curious. And he couldn't stop wanting to lay his hands all over her curvaceous body. Or wanting to kiss that small but potent mouth again, or thrust his fingers through that thick mass of chestnut-colored curls, tugging them aside to allow his mouth full access to the long, delectable nape of her neck.

Do it. Say it. Tell her what you want.

"Eden," he said, surprised at how raspy his voice sounded. "I'm going to lay my cards on the table."

She moistened her lips with the tip of her tongue. "Yes?"

"Alec Ramsey!" a masculine voice cut through the sexual tension like tungsten steel.

Startled, they both jerked their heads toward the man who'd approached their table when they weren't paying attention.

"Yes?"

Alec didn't recognize the muscular guy in his early twenties but apparently the man recognized him. From the looks of his clothes and his privileged carriage Alec pegged him as a trust-fund baby who was trying hard to come across as hip and streetwise. A diamond-studded young woman barely out of her teens hovered at his elbow.

"Jeff Brockman." He thrust his hand toward Alec. Alec shook the guy's hand. "Have we met?"

"Not formally no, but I'm a huge fan. I have every issue of *Single Guy* ever published and I follow your amateur extreme sports career. I was at the Banff snowboarding competition when you did the one-eighty-to-fakie and ended up bonking a trash can. Even though you got disqualified, totally awesome performance, man."

"You a boarder?"

"Dude, I'm so there."

Alec wished the guy would buzz off, but he forced himself to remain polite. "That's great."

"Man, do you have any idea how much you've influenced my life? I follow the advice in your magazine religiously and I get chicks like crazy." Jeff jerked at thumb at his date. "Check out Tiffany here. Pretty hot and tempting, huh?"

Alec smiled and nodded at the woman. Tiffany wriggled her fingers at him and winked in open invitation, letting him know all he had to do was crook a pinky finger and she'd ditch the trust-fund snowboarder without a backward glance. Alec kept his fingers completely flattened against the leg of his trousers.

"Any time a chick starts pressuring me for commitment, I drop 'em like a stone," Jeff continued. "I'm a lone wolf, ya know."

"Well, Jeff, it's been really nice meeting you, but our meal is getting cold."

"Gotcha." Jeff raised his thumb and pointed his

finger like a gun. "Lunch at a slick restaurant with a hot babe and then it's back to your place for a little sumpin' sumpin', right?"

"Right." Alec loaded his voice with sarcasm but Jeff didn't pick up on it.

"Later, dude." Jeff flashed him the Hawaiian hang loose sign. "Keep shreddin' the slopes."

"You too."

"Let's go, Tiff, I'm ready for a little sumpin' sumpin' myself."

The minute the couple left the dining room, Alec returned his attention to Eden. Her ardor had definitely cooled. In fact, her arms were crossed over her chest and a caustic look rode her lips.

"Nice readership."

"He's just one guy. Young and immature."

"I notice you didn't set him straight about the little sumpin' sumpin'."

"Look, it's all part of my public persona." Alec flashed her his most charming grin, but she wasn't buying it. "It's just business. My fans like to think I'm out there getting action twenty-four-seven."

"What about my reputation?"

He had a feeling he'd just stepped into one of those no-win situations. Hell, how had he let his happen? He should have set Jeff straight, but his macho ego had landed him squarely in trouble.

"I'm sorry. It was wrong of me to let Jeff think you and I were having an affair," he said contritely.

Her expression softened a little. "Apology accepted."

"But I'm not going to lie to you. The reason I didn't set Jeff straight is because I *want* to take you back to my apartment and spend the rest of the afternoon making love to you."

"Would you now?"

"There's just one thing."

"Oh?"

"I can't promise you anything."

"Does that mean you can't promise me an orgasm?"

"Actually, sweetheart," he drawled. "I can pretty much promise you an orgasm, but that's about it. What I meant to say is that I want you. I find you incredibly attractive and I'd love to get to know you better. But I'm a confirmed bachelor. Marriage isn't in the stars for me. In fact, as you just witnessed, my livelihood is based on my image as a single man. So if you're looking for something long-term I need to know now, before we start down this road. I like you too much to hurt you."

"You certainly think a lot of yourself, don't you?"

"What?" Her question took him aback.

"Do you think I'm some gushy little groupie like Tiffany who can't wait to steal your underwear for a souvenir and doodle 'I heart Alec' all over my notebook?"

"No, that's not what I think of you at all. I'm saying this badly. What I mean is that I'm open to a mutually beneficial sexual relationship if you are. A no-strings-attached fling."

Mentally he groaned as he heard the words come

out of his own mouth. What was the matter with him? Normally he wasn't this inept at seduction. Something about Eden caused him to stick his foot in his mouth at every turn. If she slapped his face right now, he wouldn't blame her.

In fact, when she leaned across the table toward him, he flinched.

But she didn't slap him.

Instead, she reached over and plucked a stray thread from her red sweater off the lapel of his black jacket.

"Too late," she murmured. "You already had a string attached."

He laughed nervously. "Well? What do you say? Want to explore this chemistry between us?"

She paused for the longest moment, sizing him up, that red sweater string snared between her index finger and the pad of her thumb. Just when he was about to beg her to say something, she spoke.

"Hmm, I don't think so."

"No?" Damn, why did he have to sound so disappointed? "May I ask why not?"

"You worry me, Ramsey." She drummed her fingers on the stem of her wineglass.

"Worry you? How do I worry you?"

"Either you're the most arrogant man I've ever met or…"

"Or what?"

She shook her head. "Never mind. No doubt my first impressions were correct. You're probably just very arrogant."

He wasn't arrogant. Was he?

He touched her arm. "No, please, spill it. I want to hear what's on your mind."

"Well…" She dragged out the word, the saucy gleam in her eyes provoking him. "You've made such a production of telling me you're not into commitment that I've got to wonder what you're afraid of."

"Afraid? I'm not afraid of anything," he denied, but at the same time his lips were flapping, his knees were quaking. "What do I have to be afraid of?"

She rubbed the sweater thread between her finger and thumb, slipped him a Mona Lisa smile and whispered, "Strings."

"DO YOU THINK I'm arrogant?" Alec asked as he slammed the blue rubber ball against the back wall of the racquetball court with an echoing *thwack.*

He and Randy Sterling were playing at the exclusive Gentlemen's Gym on the Upper East Side, where they both held a lifetime membership courtesy of Uncle Mac. Two days had passed since his frustrating lunch date with Eden and he couldn't stop thinking about her or the way she'd turned him down.

You worry me, Ramsey.

He worried her? What had she meant by that? Why would she worry about him?

"She humbled you!" Randy hooted and dove for the shot, his sneakers squeaking on the waxed wooden floor of the court. "Priceless."

Alec returned the volley with a fierce backhand. ''She didn't humble me. She rejected me.''

''She called you arrogant and it bugs the hell out of you.''

''What's arrogant about being honest?''

''I'm guessing it wasn't the honesty she considered arrogant, but rather your supposition that she would find your no-strings-attached proposal irresistible.''

''I didn't mean it that way,'' Alec growled, and whacked the ball hard, channeling his frustrations to the inanimate object with gusto.

''How did you mean it?''

''A mutually beneficial arrangement where we both have a good time.''

''Look at it from her point of view. Rich, good-looking guy says, 'Hey, baby, I wanna do you and drop you like a hot potato when I get bored.' Yeah, that's an offer no woman could refuse.''

Alec glared. ''Don't get on your high horse. You used to do the same sort of thing before you met Jill.''

''I've matured. I now realize there's much more to a relationship than sex.''

''I gather Jill is still sticking to that second virginity thing until your wedding night.''

''I can handle it,'' Randy said tightly.

''Yep. I figure that's exactly what you've been doing. Handling it.'' Alec goaded him.

Randy returned the ball with such force Alec almost missed it. ''Abstinence heightens the sexual response and deepens intimacy.''

"Sounds like Jill has been reading to you from her psychology books again."

"It wouldn't kill you to learn a little more about the fairer sex."

"What?" Alec had spent the better part of his adult life learning about the fairer sex. The most popular feature in *Single Guy* was the monthly section instructing men on what it was that women wanted. And here Randy was insinuating he didn't know what he was talking about when it came to sex and romance. He was so stunned by Randy's accusation he missed the shot.

"I win." Randy gloated and threw his hands in the air. He trotted over to his gym bag sitting beside the door, pulled out a towel and proceeded to mop his face.

"You cheated. You distracted me."

"Hey, all's fair in love and racquetball."

"How about we go three out of five?"

"Can't. Jill's making dinner tonight."

"Meow." Alec said, and made a sound like a whip cracking.

Randy cut him a dirty look. "Your immature gibes no longer work on me."

"Yeah, like just because you're getting married you're suddenly Mr. Maturity."

"What can I say? Falling in love changes a guy."

"Which is precisely why you can count me out of that merry-go-round."

"You're mixing your metaphors."

"Now you're correcting my grammar? Watch out,

Sterling, next you'll be recommending a good laxative.''

"What are you so afraid of, Ramsey?"

"Me? I'm not the one who's too chicken for a racquetball rematch.''

The next team waiting for the court tapped on the outside glass and raised quizzical eyebrows.

"Anyway," Randy said, "time's up."

They picked up their belongings and left the court. Feeling vaguely unsettled, Alec stopped by the vending machine in the hallway and bought a bottle of Gatorade. Maybe his potassium was low. Maybe that's why he was feeling out of sorts.

"So what do you think I should do about Eden?" Alec asked, polishing off the Gatorade as they headed for the locker room.

"She made it clear she wasn't interested. Let it go."

"I can't let it go."

"Yeah, because you have a hard time taking no for an answer."

"The least I can do is apologize. I don't want her thinking I'm a jerk. Should I send flowers?"

"Too generic."

"You're right. I should send something more personal, but not sexually suggestive. Any ideas?"

"What's she like?"

Alec smiled, remembering. "You mean besides sexy and gorgeous?"

"Besides that."

"She's straightforward. I like that about her. Sassy.

But steady, you know. I mean here she is owning her own business and she can't be more than twenty-five.'' Alec paused. ''In a way, some of her mannerisms remind me of Kylie,'' he said, referring to his second youngest sister, the actuary who longed to fall in love but was too scared to date. The sister who'd been most deeply affected by their father's death.

''How so?''

''I have a feeling Eden's a worrywart like Kylie, but that doesn't really jibe with owning her own business. An entrepreneur has to be a risk taker.''

''Ah,'' Randy said. ''Now it comes out. That's why you're so taken with her.''

''What do you mean?''

''She's a paradox. Interesting and complex. And you, my friend, are attracted to the unusual, conflicting and attention-grabbing.''

Hmm. Good point. He literally burned with the need to know more about Eden Montgomery. A fretful entrepreneur was just loaded with intriguing conflicts. No wonder he worried her.

And then Alec had his answer. He knew exactly what he was going to send her as an apology for his graceless gaffe and see if maybe, just maybe, he could change her mind about him.

Stymied. Stumped. Stuck.

Glumly Eden stared at an empty basket and the vast array of sensual accoutrements spread out on the table, her mind a complete blank.

It had been four days since her lunch with Alec,

four miserable days in which she hadn't come up with a single creative idea. She'd also been unable to stop obsessing about what had happened.

Over and over, she relived the thwarted date, replaying her brazen kiss, his offer of no-strings-attached sex and her refusal. She'd wanted to accept his offer, more than anything in the world, but in truth, the arc of sexual awareness between them was more dangerous than a downed power line in the middle of Broadway at rush hour. That sense of danger both thrilled and scared her.

What woman in her right mind would actively court emotional electrocution?

Then again, what a way to go.

Eden sighed. She wanted him, yet she feared his potent zap of masculinity. She was also dismayed to discover that the burst of creativity she had experienced while brainstorming Randy and Jill's basket with Alec completely deserted her once she returned to the boutique.

Why was she inspired only in his presence? What was it about him that freed her mind when nothing else could? In a desperate attempt to prove to herself she didn't need him to come up with innovative ideas, Eden had spent the weekend watching blue movies, leafing through hip magazines and attending a sexually militant avant-garde art show, all to no avail. She hadn't felt turned-on once.

Face it. The downed power line is your muse.

Yipes. Muses were such fickle creatures.

"Mail call." Ashley, wearing a camouflage skirt

and T-shirt, green tights and a black beret, entered the back room, where Eden sat perched on a tall stool.

"What are you today? Guerilla chic meets Parisian café?"

"Ha-ha." Ashley stuck out her studded tongue. She carried an armful of envelopes and dumped them on the table next to a vase of feathers. "You've been quite bitchy since things didn't work out with the playboy."

"You're right. I shouldn't take my frustrations out on you." Eden reached for the mail and sorted through it. Bill, bill, bill. Junk mail. Junk mail.

"Oh," Ashley said. "I almost forgot." She reached in her pocket and drew out a small brown-paper package. "This came from Alec."

"What?" Eden leaned across the table and ripped the package from her hand.

Ashley grinned. "Maybe things went better than you thought."

Eden tore off the wrapping paper to reveal a rectangular blue box with the name of a renowned jewelry store embossed in silver on the front. Her pulse thudded loudly against her veins. Damn, if her hands weren't trembling.

She peeled off the lid and studied the contents with puzzlement.

A rock.

The man had sent her a rock.

Albeit a very pretty rock. It was oblong, slightly wider and longer than the width and breadth of her thumb, primarily deep emerald-green shot through with black and lighter green swirls complex as a fingerprint. In fact, there was an indentation curved into the rock where her thumb nestled an exact fit.

The stone was glass smooth and cool. When she lifted it to her nose, she smelled the fresh, faint scent of a river trickling through her mind.

She caressed the indentation with her thumb, memorizing the avocado dip of it. Rhythmically she stroked and was surprised to find her body relaxing, her mind sharply focusing on the effortless glide over the surface.

"What is it?" Ashley asked, peering over Eden's shoulder and disrupting her calm mood.

Eden held out the stone.

"Hmm. Looks like the rocks my brother used to spin in his rock tumbler. Except for the thumb imprint."

Eden looked down at the box and realized a note had been tucked under the stone. She plucked out the folded piece of paper and opened it up.

Dear Eden,
Please accept my apology. You were right. I behaved like an arrogant jerk. I hope this worry stone helps to alleviate your worries about me.
Alec

A worry stone?

An odd please-forgive-me gift that caused a flutter of an unidentified emotion to tighten her chest. Not so much because of the silly superstition—imagine, being able to simply rub your worries into the stone—but because Alec had uncannily honed in on her greatest flaw and offered her an instant cure-all.

And then she named the feeling restlessly rolling through her. A co-mingling of desire, forgiveness, hope and...*expectation.*

He'd cared enough to make the gesture and not just any gesture. He could have sent a card or flowers or some other standard token, but instead he had read her signals, deduced her chief insecurity and tailored his gift to fit her needs.

She was touched.

"What is it?" Ashley repeated, picking up the stone and turning it over in her hand.

"A worry stone. You rub it to wash your worries away."

"Boy, has this guy got you pegged." Ashley eyed her. "Don't tell me you went into a worst-case scenario spiel with him."

"No, I did not." She held out a palm. "May I have it back, please?"

Ashley dropped the stone into her hand.

The telephone at the front desk jangled.

"I'll get it," Ashley said and scurried into the other room, leaving Eden to thoughtfully massage the stone.

"For you," Ashley hollered a minute later. "Tori Drake from Spice-Up-Your-Love-Life Cruises."

Oh dear, Eden fretted. Spice-Up-Your-Love-Life Cruises was her biggest account. Hadn't the baskets she'd shipped last week gotten there in time?

Calm down.

She dropped the stone into her pocket and went to take the receiver from Ashley. "Hello, Tori."

"Eden, good morning. How are you?"

"Fine. Did you get the baskets I sent?" Nervously she ran her thumb over the stone.

"Yes, and that's why I'm calling."

"Is there a problem? Were they damaged in shipping?"

"No. The contents are fine." An awkward pause followed.

"Yes?"

"Eden, these baskets aren't up to your usual caliber of work."

Oh dear. She'd been right to worry. "Tori, I'm really sorry. How can I make it right?" She wouldn't offer an excuse. Her creative block wasn't Tori's problem.

"We'll accept them this time, Eden, but I must warn you, we've been approached by another designer whose baskets are a lot edgier."

"Edgier?"

"Hip. Contemporary. You know *Real Sex* and *Taxicab Confessions* edgy. Naughty, saucy, flaunt-it-if-you've-got it, in-your-face raw and randy."

"I see." What the hell did *that* mean?

"Eden, you've been an excellent supplier. And up until the last couple of shipments your product has been excellent."

"But..."

"Unless you can put together something that will

wow the pants off the executives, I'm afraid we're going to have to switch to the new designer.''

Every worst-case-scenario fear she'd ever had came crashing in upon her. The money she made from Spice-Up-Your-Love-Life Cruises paid her basic essentials. Without it, she would be in deep financial trouble.

Don't panic, rub the stone.

Miraculously, rubbing the stone did calm her. Okay. All right. She could deal with this.

But you're creatively blocked, whispered her naysaying voice.

She rubbed faster. She could get unblocked. If all else failed, she knew where to find her muse.

"Eden? Are you there?"

"Yes, Tori, I'm here."

"You have until the end of the month to come up with something.''

"Thank you for giving me the opportunity to improve," Eden said, breathing a sigh of relief. Thank heavens, it was the first week of October.

"I'm looking forward to seeing what you come up with," Tori said. "I know you won't let us down.''

Gee, no pressure there.

"I won't," she assured her.

"Good luck." Tori said, and rang off.

Eden depressed the switch hook with her index finger, but did not cradle the phone. For the longest time she simply stood staring at the receiver.

Come on, you know what you have to do. What you

secretly yearn to do. You want him and you know it and he wants you. What's wrong with that?

But how would he react to her scar?

You'll never know until you try.

Besides, what choice did she have? Her creativity had disappeared like smoke up a flue the minute she was separated from Alec. If she hoped to salvage the Spice-Up-Your-Love-Life account she knew what she must do, stomach butterflies or not.

Gently fondling the worry stone, she rehearsed the speech in her head. This good girl was determined to go bad in a very splashy way.

Taking a deep breath, she took the plunge and punched in Alec's phone number.

"*Single Guy* magazine," said a clipped, professional male voice.

"May I speak with Alec Ramsey?" Eden asked, amazed at how peaceful she felt once she had made her decision.

"Whom may I say is calling?"

"Eden Montgomery."

"And this is regarding...?"

"An order Mr. Ramsey placed with me for his friend's wedding."

"Oh," the assistant said. "You're her. The gift basket woman."

"That would be me," she admitted.

"Alec is in a meeting, but he wouldn't want to miss your call." He put her on hold and Eden waited, surprised to find herself growing bolder by the minute.

Maybe there was something magical about that

worry stone. She was already feeling more imaginative, more inspired as she thought about exactly how this would play out.

"Eden," Alec's breathless voice spilled into her ear a few seconds later. "Did you get my gift?"

"Yes," she purred, determined to sound as sexy as possible. "It was very thoughtful of you."

"I'm glad you like it."

Silence descended, but only for a moment. If she hesitated, Eden feared her courage would disappear and she'd back out.

Can't back out. You need him in order to save the Spice-Up-Your-Love-Life account.

She grabbed the bull by the horns. "Alec," she whispered. "I have a very indecent proposal."

6

"HERE'S MY LIST of stipulations," Eden dared, thrilling to the fact she was bold enough to demand what she wanted from him.

Alec had eagerly agreed to meet her in Central Park at noon. The sky was flat and gray, but Central Park itself was alive with color. The grass was still a rich, country-club green while the trees gaily waved red and gold leaves. They were seated side by side on a bench while joggers sprinted by. Mothers and nannies pushed strollers. Pigeons strutted, bobbing their heads in search of dropped food. The autumn panorama was breathtaking, but not nearly as breathtaking as the man sitting beside her.

He gave her an endearing, lopsided grin. "You've got a list of stipulations?"

"Well, not an actual physical, written-down list," she admitted. "It's all in my head."

"Okay then." He draped an arm across the bench behind her. "Let's hear it."

Eden cleared her throat and forced herself to meet his bemused gaze. "You're making fun of me."

"I'm not."

"Stop grinning."

"I can't. I'm just so damned happy you called."

"Really?"

The look he shot her way was heated and meaningful. "Really."

"All right then, stipulation one. The affair will last for four weeks and four weeks only. No renegotiating this point." Eden struggled to keep her voice low, steady and unemotional. It would ruin everything if he guessed she wasn't cool, calm and completely in control of her feelings. She had instituted this particular rule simply to protect herself. She knew that if she wasn't careful she could fall hard for him. "Do you agree?"

"The next four weeks is about pushing the limits of our sexuality. And at the end of the month…" He hesitated and then said huskily, "It's over."

Was she being hypervigilant or did he actually sound dubious, as if he didn't really believe the words he'd just uttered. But why would he hesitate? He'd made sure she understood he wasn't the marrying kind.

"Two," she continued. "No meeting each other's friends or family. No going to each other's apartments. No dating. Nothing personal. Nothing lasting. Just hot, delicious sex."

"Are you sure that's what you want?"

"Absolutely."

"All right." He nodded. His jaw tensed tight, his smoky-gray eyes practically vibrating with excitement.

She was excited, too. Thrilled. Delighted. Ecstatic.

She was going after what she wanted, what she needed. It felt shockingly good and dangerous and naughty as all get-out.

This wasn't about love or finding a mate. This affair was about expanding her sexual horizons in order to boost her creativity. This was about discovering her body's response to sexual pleasure so that she no longer felt like a hypocrite when she designed her baskets. But, ultimately, this affair was about boosting her self-esteem and conquering her shame over her burn scars.

Which led Eden to her third stipulation. In order for this to work, she had to trust Alec completely. It took time to build trust. Time she didn't have. So she had devised a plan to escalate their intimacy while easing into sex.

He trailed a finger over her shoulder.

"Three," she said, steeling herself not to shiver and give away her vulnerability. "I want to start slow and build the tension. I want this to be an affair to remember. I want to play games."

Alec audibly gulped. "Games?"

"Fantasy role-playing games. Bold sheik and willing harem captive. Biker chick and straitlaced businessman. Doctor and nurse."

God, how she wanted this. To actually live out the adventures she'd spent years dreaming up for other people. It was time for *her* fantasies to come true.

"Like your baskets," he murmured so low she could barely hear him.

"Exactly."

He didn't have to know she was on a desperate search for new ideas. For something wild and edgy and in-your-face. He didn't need to find out that she was using him to kick-start her creativity.

"Will there be toys?" he asked devilishly.

"Oh yes, there will be toys." She grinned, tickled to find him quickly sinking into the spirit of things. "We will meet two nights a week. Tuesdays and Saturdays are good for me, but that's open for your approval."

"I'll clear my calendar," he said. "Tomorrow is Tuesday." His voice was a silky slide of pleasure in her ears. His knees bumped hers and his lips hovered perilously close to her mouth. "We start then?"

"Yes," she said. "Meet me at the Grand Duchess hotel in the lobby at seven o'clock. And be prepared for anything."

SWALLOWING HARD, Eden dropped her bathrobe to the floor. She studied her nakedness in the full-length mirror. Mostly, she tried not to notice her body. She got in and out of the shower without turning her head toward the looking glass. She put on her clothes as quickly as possible. She never, ever slept in the nude.

But now she had to look, had to view her scar with fresh eyes. Had to see herself the way a stranger would see her.

Gingerly she ran a hand down her abdomen and fingered the pink, uneven edges of the burn scar that started directly below her belly button and ran parallel with her hipbones. The scar widened, flaring out to encompass her entire pelvic girdle and three inches down the tops of her thighs. Her pubic hair, which that been singed off in the fire, had never grown back.

She was as bald as a hairless Chihuahua.

How's that for edgy, Tori. She tilted her head and turned slightly for a three-quarter view.

A full Brazilian bikini wax wouldn't have produced a muff this bare. Eden gave a sharp bark of laughter at the notion of women paying lots of money to achieve the same slick look. What she wouldn't give to have her hair back. She missed the dark, curly trouser tresses.

Face facts. Upon first sight, anyone would find her pink, stark mons unsettling.

Josh had certainly been unsettled. Correction. He'd been shocked.

Eden tried to squelch the memory but it rose up anyway. It had happened a year ago, but her shame stung as vividly as if the rejection had been yesterday.

It was her fourth date with Josh and they'd been getting along really well. They liked the same music, read the same books and enjoyed the same restaurants. She'd only been mildly attracted to him sexually, but she'd had two glasses of wine over dinner and her resistance was done. When he'd suggested they end the night in her apartment, she'd thought why not?

The thing was, he knew about the fire. She'd told him about her wounds and the surgeries; still he hadn't been prepared.

He'd actually gagged when he'd seen her scar. He went from erect to flaccid in five seconds flat.

"I'm sorry, Eden," he'd said, quickly sliding off her bed. She'd scrambled to throw the blankets over her nakedness, stunned to think he'd found her so repulsive. "I tried to keep an open mind about this but—" he had slapped a palm over his mouth "—I can't."

And then he'd literally run from her apartment.

Eden brushed a tear from the corner of her eye. *Stop crying over that jerk.*

But what if Alec felt the same way? What if he was unable to look past her disfigurement?

Fear clutched her.

She couldn't do it. She couldn't go through with this seduction. She was all bluff and false bravado.

"I can't," she spoke to her reflection.

You have to. You need him to get unblocked. To save your biggest account.

"No more pain," she whimpered. "I couldn't bear it if he rejects me, too."

Of course that was the reason she'd insisted on the role-playing games and taking things step-by-step. To make absolutely certain she could trust him not to react negatively. But she couldn't do this alone. She needed help. Emotional support. Encouragement.

Jayne. She would know what to do. Eden picked up the phone and called her sexually adventurous friend for advice.

Be prepared for anything.

Eden's parting words circled in his head. A dare, a

challenge, a call to adventure. Did she have any idea how she'd piqued his interest and stirred his blood? His curiosity was aroused; his body prickled with heightened anticipation.

She was an erotic mastermind.

Alec sat perched on a camelback sofa in the lobby of the elegant Grand Duchess Hotel on Tuesday evening, his hip pocket filled with condoms, his fingers nervously drumming against his kneecap.

For the ninety-ninth time in the span of ten minutes, he checked his watch. Seven minutes after seven. Where was she? Had he been stood up?

A flash of red on the sidewalk outside the window caught his attention and Alec turned his head for a better look.

The big-haired blonde strutted down the sidewalk, all sass and spicy attitude. She wore a stretchy blouse so low-cut it oughta be illegal, and her glorious, look-fellas-no-bra breasts bounced high with each step she took.

A tight red skirt hugged her curvaceous hips. She stalked on stilettos so tall he wondered how she managed to keep her balance. Her gorgeous gams were shod in a pair of scarlet stockings so touchable his fingers ached.

The blond vixen hurried up the steps of the Grand Duchess and entered the revolving door. Every masculine head within eyeshot turned to stare. Something familiar nagged. Did he know her? She passed through the door and then turned left into the lobby and swaggered straight for him.

Realization dawned.

Holy cow, Eden!

In a blond wig.

Looking decidedly like a hooker.

Spellbound, his jaw unhinged. Adrenaline pumped through his veins. Testosterone flowed.

She ignored his stare. In fact, she ignored him completely.

And that was erotic, too!

Instead she walked over, eased down on the opposite end of the sofa and crossed her legs at the knees. She tousled her hair with her hand—a hand sporting three-inch-long fake crimson fingernails and jangly bracelets too numerous to count.

"Eden?" he whispered, flustered by her transformation and mightily turned-on.

"Name's Lola, buddy. Not that it's any of your beeswax," she said in nasally New Jersey accent. "Unless, that is, you got a wad of cash money in your pocket."

He identified the game. Thrilled to it. He was delighted and even a little scared at how she'd so completely assumed her role.

"How much?" he asked huskily.

Finally she looked at him, angling him a haughty glance down the length of her nose. "You a cop?"

"No, no, not a cop."

"You sure?"

He nodded vigorously.

"Three hundred for the night."

"Three hundred! Isn't that a bit steep?"

"Hey mister, you get what you pay for."

"And you're worth three hundred dollars?" He was so excited his hands trembled. She leaned in closer, swaying and jiggling and revealing not only lots of cleavage, but also a small red heart tattooed on her left breast. Eden had a tattoo?

Alec realized then how little he knew about her and that realization served to send his desire soaring even higher.

"You have no idea." Her wicked grin sent a shaft of exquisitely painful desire blasting through his groin.

"Are you wearing underwear?" He dropped his voice and at first he wasn't sure she'd heard him.

A heartbeat passed.

She slid him a look that jammed his libido into hyperdrive. A suggestive look that declared, *I'm thinking of something very dirty and if you do things my way you won't regret it.* But just as easily the expression could have said, *I've got a switchblade in my purse and I'm not afraid to use it.*

Then she relaxed her mouth, slightly parted her lushly painted lips and slipped her tongue between her teeth in a gesture so provocative he almost shot his load right then and there.

"No," she purred, low and throaty. "No underwear here. Are you interested or not?"

His gaze locked on her thighs, his mind racing as he imagined the treats that awaited him on the other side of that skirt.

"I don't have three hundred dollars," he said, playing along.

"If you don't have the cash, stop wasting my time." She stood.

"Wait, wait." He reached out a hand to touch her wrist. The minute he made contact, Alec's hand sizzled and burned. "What can I get for a hundred?"

She crooked a finger at him. "Come with me."

Surprised that he could even put one foot in front of another, Alec removed his jacket and held it in front of him to hide his gigantic erection. With his gaze locked on her beautiful butt, he followed her to the elevators.

He'd never experienced excitement like this. Not skydiving or mountain climbing or racing motorcycles. How extraordinary.

The sense of reckless abandon pushed him headlong into self-indulgent excesses with this stunning woman. If he lived to be a hundred, he would never forget her.

The elevator settled with a muted ding and the doors whispered open. People got off and then Eden took his hand and led him inside.

With one of those long, dangerous fingernails, she lightly trailed a line up the inside of his forearm. Who would have ever thought a gentle scratch would feel so incredible? Her touch blasted a whole new level of awareness through his body as he imagined those hard-tipped fingernails exploring other more tender parts.

The elevator stopped on the eighth floor and she led him to the end of the hallway. She extracted a key card from her purse. Tresses from her long blond wig fell forward over her shoulder as she bent to slip the card into the door handle.

Her bold sexual confidence belied the reticence that had led her to reject him at the French restaurant. She was a complex and complicated woman with obviously two strong but opposing impulses that drove her. He wanted to know what they were. That hungry curiosity nearly shoved him over the edge of reason. He couldn't wait to see what she had in store for him.

She'd started this strange dance, this mesmerizing game, but damn if he wasn't committed to finishing it.

After turning the doorknob, she stepped over the threshold and flicked on the light. "You comin'?" she asked, staying in character with her street-tough accent.

"Uh-huh." He hustled inside and the door automatically snapped closed behind him.

In the muted glow of lamplight, his gaze raked over the tight clothes, emphasizing every shape and contour of her body. His eyes flicked from her breasts to her legs to her butt and back again.

"Like what you see?" she asked tartly.

"Very much."

"If you want to see more, you've got to show me the money." She crossed her arms over her chest and tapped a foot.

The woman could have been an actress, she was that damned good. Feeling for all the world like a sheepish john paying for the favors of a lady of the night, Alec pried his wallet from his back pocket and took out a hundred-dollar bill.

She plucked the money from his hand and tucked it down the front of her blouse, where Benjamin Franklin ended up nestled next to the rose tattoo.

"Take off your shirt," she said, plunking down in a chair, crossing her knees and swinging her leg provocatively.

"I thought you were going to show me more."

"You first."

Alec tossed his jacket on the dresser and then unbuttoned his shirt cuffs. His fingers migrated to the buttons at his throat and he was surprised to find he felt weirdly ambivalent about this and sort of shy. It was an alien sensation and he wasn't sure he liked it.

But he did like the frankly sexual gleam in her eyes as she watched him strip off his shirt.

"Nice pecs," she observed. "You work out?"

"Yes."

"Most of my customers are old and flabby," she said. She got to her feet and moved across the room toward him. Alec's heart went thumpa-thumpa-thumpa with each undulation of her hips. "You don't look like the type of guy who has to pay for sex."

"I want it anonymous," he murmured. "Illicit and illegal."

"Then you've come to the right place." She

stopped just inches from his face. In an impulsive move, she lifted her mouth to his chin and bit him.

Not hard, but not so soft, either.

And then she poked him lightly in the chest with a fingernail and raked it over the planes of his naked muscles.

Alec muffled a groan. His erection burgeoned and his knees weakened.

Chill out. Calm down, man, or you won't last five seconds.

"How'd you get this?" She purred, following the curve of an old crescent-shaped scar two inches to the right of his nipple.

"Climbing 2K."

"For real? You climbed 2K?"

"I didn't make it to the top."

"Stopped prematurely, didja?"

"The injury…" His eyes locked with hers.

"And this one?" She ran her fingernail over the small but deep jagged scar dug into his left bicep.

"Motocross."

"Did you win?"

He shook his head. "Didn't finish."

"Hmm," she said. "I see a pattern developing here. Do you have problems finishing what you start, John?"

None too gently, he pulled her into his arms. "Those were just my failures. Wait until you hear about my successes. You should have seen me laying pipe on the North shore of Oahu last year."

"Ooh, laying pipe. I like the sound of that one. But Ben doesn't buy that kind of time." She patted the hundred-dollar bill nestled between her breasts. "Let's stop talking and get down to business."

God, he loved this game. She was simply amazing.

And then, before he knew what she was planning, her hands were at his belt, undoing the buckle.

He hissed in his breath as she pulled the belt through the loops with a leathery slither and aggressively two-stepped him backward toward the bed. She splayed a palm against the center of his chest and butt-planted him onto the bedspread.

His mouth was like wet carpet, his stomach a bowling ball. He felt exactly the same way he had the time he and Randy had base-jumped off the hard granite cliff of Kjerag, Norway, with a stinging cold breeze in his face, a rig on his back and the knowledge that very shortly he'd be leaping off the edge of a very large abyss.

He was committed.

Eden climbed over him, straddling his body. She was breathing as hard and fast as he, her nimble fingers working the zipper of his pants, assiduously trying to free his erection.

"Eden," he moaned.

"Not Eden," she said sharply. "Lola."

"Lola," he whispered, as she shucked both his pants and his briefs over his hips in one fluid movement and flung them to the floor. "Lola."

He wanted to touch her, wanted to get her naked,

wanted to feel her hot, damp skin pressed flush against his.

But Lola had other ideas.

Her hands were wrapped around his stiff cock and he could barely breathe, much less think. One hand rhythmically stroked his shaft, while the other hand manipulated the head of his penis with soft, teasing caresses.

Around and around, she swirled. Up and down. A tantalizing, mind-blowing blend of expert maneuvers that had him wondering how she knew so well the secrets of a man's body. When she tickled his balls he thought he was going to lose his mind with lust.

"You're one naughty, nasty lady," he growled through clenched teeth.

"Yeah, baby, talk dirty to me."

He told her then, in very graphic terms what he ached to do to her.

Yes, yes, yes. This was exactly what he wanted. A free fall. He wanted to plummet into her and forget everything.

Except he didn't have the chance.

Lola increased the intensity of the strokes, pushing him closer, ever closer to the edge. He lost all ability to think, to even move from his spread-eagle position on the bed. He felt the orgasm building and building and building, hard, hot and unstoppable.

He was lost. Gone. Adrift in ecstasy.

"Aaaa," he cried out. Invisible wind screamed through his ears. His body arched in an involuntarily response. The room spun, whizzing past him, a visual explosion of light, color and sound.

Megarush!

A split second later the essence of him splurged into her hand and he drifted on a smooth canopy of release.

Delicately she took a tissue from the box beside the nightstand and cleaned him up.

Blindly Alec reached for her, determined to recover as quickly as possible and give to her what she had just given to him and much, much more.

But Lola slipped from his grasp. She got to her feet, dropped the tissue in the wastebasket and headed for the door.

"Wait, wait. That's it? You're leaving?"

She stopped, cocked her head back over her shoulder at him and winked. "See you Saturday, stud. Same time. Same place. Different game."

7

INVIGORATED, Eden worked far into the night on a prototype gift basket for Spice-Up-Your-Love-Life Cruises. Her mind spun out of control with a thousand forbidden fantasies as image upon image expanded, unfolded and grew.

She felt as if she were capturing lightning in a bottle, casting her mind back to what had just happened between her and Alec and then translating that experience into concrete, workable art. The sense of excitement carried her steadily upward on an innovative high.

Filled with driving inspiration after she left Alec at the Grand Duchess, she hadn't even bothered to go home and change. At one o'clock in the morning, she sat in the back room at Wickedly Wonderful still dressed in her Happy Hooker outfit, Alec's one-hundred-dollar bill stuffed coyly down her cleavage beside the stick-on rose tattoo.

She would put the money toward the balance he owed on Jill and Randy's gift basket. In the meantime, a shiver of sinful delight raced up her spine every time she thought about how she'd daringly exchanged sexual favors for money.

It didn't get much edgier than that and the pulse-throbbing encounter was the stimulation for this new basket.

"You were awesome," she whispered to herself.

Jayne would have been proud that she'd so successfully utilized her boudoir expertise. Even now, simply thinking about how she'd taken control and brought Alec to orgasm caused her hands to tremble.

She'd tested the limits of her courage, brought a man to his knees with her sexual techniques, dislodged her creative roadblock and still managed to keep her emotions out of the fray.

Except now, she ached for more. She wanted more than just an artistic boost. She wanted sex and lots of it. Tonight, she had gotten a taste of her own feminine power.

Eden caught a glimpse of herself in the shoplifting mirror mounted on the wall between the back room and the main part of the store. Her hair, stripped free of the blond wig, was a wild tumble down her shoulders. An untamed expression of smug satisfaction curled the corners of her lips and she found she could not stop smiling.

She simply couldn't wait to go back for more.

A HUNDRED-DOLLAR hand job.

Alec could not stop thinking about what had happened at the Grand Duchess. All morning long he'd sat in his office mooning over Eden. He had been so uninvolved in the day's business, Holden came to stand in the doorway three separate times to ask him if he was feeling okay.

Although he'd assured his assistant he was fine, Alec was far from okay. He'd been ambushed, bush-whacked, surprise-attacked, and he had loved every damned second of it.

Eden Montgomery far exceeded his expectations. She was beyond naughty. The woman was a virtual firecracker sending him into orbit with her advanced pyrotechnics. He tried to tell himself he was over-stating the case, that last night had been so incredible simply because it had been a long time since he'd been with a woman, but he couldn't deny the truth.

Everything about her appealed to him. Her sexy-yet-sweet scent, the fact that he knew very little about her, her earthy voice and her ability to change like a chameleon.

Plus, her scintillating sex games drove him wild.

She had teased him, pleased him, and then she had walked out the door. Her disappearing act drove him nuts. Why had she gone to such lengths to seduce him with her salacious call-girl foreplay only to leave before she'd had her turn?

Was it all part of some master plan to blow his ever-loving mind?

He couldn't wait to get his hands on her again. He was antsy to unearth her secret fantasies and serve them up to her on a platter. A shudder passed through him as he recalled the feel of her fingers on his body, and he had to close his eyes and concentrate to fight off an erection.

Eden's early departure had simply whetted his appetite, which he supposed was exactly what she'd intended. But come Saturday night, he was going to the Grand Duchess fully prepared to turn the tables on her.

THE NEXT TWO WEEKS PASSED in a blur of sensuous pleasure. Eden alternated between seeking Jayne's expert advice on exactly how to please her new lover and putting those brilliant techniques into operation.

At work, she labored over her newly inspired gift baskets. Her customers commented on the improvements and orders picked up.

And she owed it all to Alec.

Shamelessly he indulged her, giving her any and everything she asked for.

Except one.

He refused to allow her to bring him to orgasm again until she let him make her come. "No more of this one-sided stuff," he growled.

But Eden had declined to get naked in front of him. Partly because she still didn't trust him not to bolt at the sight of her scars and partly because the long, drawn-out seduction was so damned thrilling. Once they consummated their spiraling lust, she feared it would ruin the sexual tension.

"Wait," she'd insisted. "Wait."

And so, they both suffered. Twice a week they met to up the stakes with their sex games, the ante growing with each new encounter as they teased and taunted, dragging out the suspense while tugging each other to the edge of insanity and beyond.

Ah, sweet torture.

They watched soft-core dirty movies together and Eden read to him from books of erotic poetry. They kissed and fondled each other through their clothing. Her imagination detonated and her games became increasingly more titillating.

She invented foot-fetish night, complete with foot massages, pedicures and the most mind-blowing sensation she'd experienced to date—toe sucking. Who knew having your toes licked and sucked and rubbed would unearth an entire minefield of erogenous zones? The soles, the heel, the Achilles tendon, all tingled and throbbed and begged for attention.

And when she slid her tongue between his fresh, clean toes and boldly nibbled with a light pressure, Alec actually came. Knowing she could do that to him just by licking his feet made her feel desirable and powerful and fully in charge of her sexuality.

Hanky-panky picnic night was Alec's idea. They rented *9 1/2 Weeks* and then ordered a wide variety of take-out foods delivered to their room at the Grand Duchess. They fed each other pepperoni pizza with their fingers, nurturing their developing appetites. They let the sweet, sticky juices from plump strawberries drip over their hands and down from their mouths.

They lingered over each and every morsel of food, savoring the flavoring, describing to each other the different tastes and contrasting textures. Sweet and sour. Hot and cold. Soft and crunchy. She'd never focused so intently on food before.

Alec leaned her head back and dropped grapes into her mouth. The fruit made a satisfying plop-plop sound against her tongue.

Eden wafted a carton of Kung Pow Chicken under his nose, urging him to inhale the peppery aroma.

They involved every sense organ in their picnic. Smearing honey and chocolate on their chests and then licking it off. Sucking sake through a straw and getting tipsy. Touching lips through the hole in a doughnut and then eating up the yeasty treat. When their teeth clacked together, they giggled like children.

All night long they kissed, and ended up falling asleep in each other's arms. They woke the next morning, spooned together and happily sated even though they had not had sex.

And on Thursdays they started calling each other for phone-sex night. This was when they slaked their desires by pleasuring themselves while they breathed hot and heavy over the phone lines, spelling out their sexual fantasies in explicit detail.

Eden could scarcely believe how far she had come in such a short time, dropping her reserve and letting herself go. Soon now, she'd be ready to take the next step and make love with Alec. The time had come. They only had two weeks left.

Eagerly she made plans for the upcoming Saturday. She bought a crotchless, black, opaque cat-suit that covered her body except for the mysterious slit in just the right location and a pair of slinky, can't-keep-your-hands-off-me, black thigh-high boots.

She stocked up on condoms, ordered champagne to be waiting in their room at the Grand Duchess and packed a bag of sexual toys.

For the rest of the week, she went around humming *Tonight's the Night.*

"WE'VE GOT TO DO SOMETHING to get them together outside of the bedroom," Jayne told Sarah as they took their lunch break together. "Eden is so determined not to fall in love that she set up some pretty insurmountable stipulations."

"Stipulations?" Sarah noshed her turkey sandwich and eyed Jayne thoughtfully.

"Eden has forbidden them to have a real date. They can't meet each other's friends or family and she insists they not go to each other's apartments. And she's put a time limit on their affair. One month and no more."

"Hmm, that is a problem."

"She's just scared to really trust a man," Jayne said. "I think it goes back to never having known her father and being abandoned by her gadabout mother."

"Alec is scared, too. He's so afraid that he's going to miss out on something wonderful if he commits to one thing or one person. He wants to keep all his options open. What he doesn't seem to realize is that if he slowed down and focused on one person or one thing, his life would be so much richer and fulfilling."

"They need to get to know each other on a personal level for their romance to bloom. Any ideas on how we get them over this hurdle?'' Jayne arched her eyebrows and blew across a spoonful of clam chowder to cool it.

''I'm hosting Jill and Randy's wedding shower at my house on Saturday afternoon. Any chance of getting Eden to Connecticut?''

Jayne made a face. ''Saturday is her busiest day at the boutique.''

''How about I have Randy contrive to get Alec away from New York so he can't pick up the basket and he'll have to ask Eden to deliver it.''

''But she would just send Ashley.''

''Unless we enlist Ashley's help.'' Sarah grinned. ''Get her to call in sick or something.''

''That could work, but what then? Eden delivers the basket and leaves.''

''You just get her to Connecticut.'' Sarah winked. ''I'll take it from there.''

BECAUSE ASHLEY HAD CALLED in sick and she had no one else to send, Eden was forced to close the shop early in order to deliver Alec's gift basket to his sister's home in Connecticut. Even with closing the store early, more than likely she would end up running late for her date with Alec.

To compensate for lost time, she'd gone ahead and dressed in the daring outfit she'd put together for their evening of unbridled lust. A black crotchless opaque body stocking that hid her scars, topped by a tight black skirt. She buttoned up a long black duster over the whole ensemble and wore the black leather boots with three-inch heels.

When Alec had called to ask if she would mind delivering the basket, her pulse had skip-hopped at the sound of his low, masculine voice.

Immediately, she had jumped to conclusions, worrying he'd phoned to cancel their date. But one stroke of the worry stone she always kept tucked in her pocket had lessened her anxiety, and when he assured her they were indeed still on for Saturday night, she'd eagerly agreed to deliver the basket, which was the silver champagne bucket they'd agreed upon for the Playboy and the Virgin theme.

Now she was regretting her decision. Here she was dressed like a wanton, taking a taxi from the train station to Sarah's house when all she wanted was to be with Alec. Of all the days for Ashley to take sick.

The taxi pulled to a stop outside a lovely two-story brick home with a perfectly manicured lawn. Clutching the heavy gift basket with both hands, Eden slid from the back seat and asked the taxi driver to wait.

She hurried up the sidewalk. Freshly fallen autumn leaves crunched beneath her boots, and the long tail of her duster slapped against the back of her legs. She rang the doorbell, fully intending to present the basket to whoever answered, then turn and head back to the taxi.

It didn't happen that way.

The minute the door opened, she found herself being hauled over the threshold and hugged by a gorgeous blonde who bore a striking resemblance to Alec.

"Come in, come in," the attractive young woman said, motioning her farther into the house. "The fun is just getting started. Everyone is in the den."

"Um, I'm just here to deliver Alec's present to the bride-to-be," Eden said. "I'm not a guest."

"Nonsense, you came all this way, you're invited. The more the merrier. I'm Sarah by the way." She extended her hand and smiled broadly.

Eden took it. "Eden Montgomery."

"Oh my! At last we meet. I absolutely loved the gift basket you made me and Zach for our wedding. I'm so glad Alec took my advice and decided to order one for Randy and Jill."

"I've got a cab waiting," Eden jerked her thumb over her shoulder. "I really can't stay."

"Come on, don't you want to see the look on Jill's face when she gets a load of that sexy basket? I know she's going to be thrilled," Sarah insisted.

"I..."

But before she had time to protest further, Sarah had taken her by the elbow and was ushering her into the den with the other guests. She introduced Eden to her good-looking husband, Zach, and then instructed him to pay Eden's cab driver and send him on his way.

"Let me take your coat," Sarah offered, holding out her hand.

"That's okay," Eden said, tightening the sash of her duster. "I'm a little chilly."

What would the women think, she wondered, if they had any idea what she was wearing?

Eden set the basket on a table piled high with gifts. She felt uncomfortable and out of place.

Oh God, what was she doing here?

The last thing she wanted was to get to know Alec's family and friends. The less she knew about him the better. A peek into his family life threatened to deliver complications she wasn't prepared to deal with.

Her relationship with Alec was a temporary one, based on the need for raunchy, illicit sex with an adventuresome man. Sex to clear her mind and dissolve her fears. Sex to reassure her that she was feminine and desirable. Sex to heal the broken places in her soul so she could move forward with her life.

Unfortunately, it seemed she wasn't about to escape the exuberant Sarah. The bubbly blonde introduced her around the room. Eden met Alec's other three sisters, Kylie, Alison and Diana, along with his mother, two aunts, a dozen female friends and the bride-to-be, Jill Fincher.

Sarah grabbed a folding chair for Eden and parked her beside the sofa next to Jill.

Jill was a lot like Alec had described her. A cool, classy brunette dressed in an understated fashion. She was quiet and reserved, but with a sharp intelligence that burned from behind her wire-framed glasses. She looked as out of place in this boisterous group of rowdy women as Eden felt.

Their gazes met. Jill smiled.

Eden smiled back and they shared an instant camaraderie.

Sarah moved to the center of the room and clapped her hands. "Ladies." She grinned. "I've got a surprise. We're all going to have our sexual fortunes told by a very gifted tea-leaf reader."

"Sexual fortunes?" Jill asked, a panicky expression crossing her face. "What's that?"

"You're going to love it." Sarah wriggled her eyebrows suggestively. "Madame Xavier's predictions are uncannily accurate. She'll tell you exactly how to keep Randy eating from the palm of your hand. She's the one who told me that Zach was going to propose when he did."

"Trust Sarah to come up with something crazy and exotic." Someone laughed.

"I can't wait," another woman said. "I need to know when this long dry spell will be over. I want sex!"

The crowd laughed.

Sarah left the room and returned with a serving cart loaded down with a teakettle and matching cups. Trailing her was a short, smiling woman who looked all the world like renowned sex therapist, Dr. Ruth. She even giggled like the famous relationship guru.

After passing out the tea, Madame Xavier instructed everyone to drink up and then to turn their cups upside down in their saucers.

"Can you believe this?" Jill leaned over and whispered to Eden. "Sarah is outrageous, but with her around there's never a dull moment. Alec is the same way. Those two are peas in a pod.''

''I'm beginning to see that.'' If she thought Sarah was outrageous, Eden wondered what Jill would think of her gift basket.

Sarah downed her tea and upended her cup into the saucer. ''To get the ball rolling,'' she said. ''I'll go first.''

Madame Xavier took the saucer, studied the tea leaves for a long moment then started giggling. ''You're wearing your husband out, Sarah. To heighten anticipation, I recommend cutting back on sex from twice a day to five times a week.''

''Ooo,'' teased the women.

Sarah proudly thrust out her chest. ''Hey, we're newlyweds, what can I say?''

''You next.'' Madame Xavier moved on to Jill.

''Me?''

Madame Xavier nodded.

Eden noticed Jill's hands trembling as she finished her tea and passed the saucer to the fortuneteller.

Madame Xavier looked at the tea-leaf patterns, and then touched her chin. She took a deep breath and Eden felt Jill tense beside her.

''Something is missing.''

''Oh.'' Jill blinked. ''I'm sorry, I accidentally swallowed a tea leaf or two.''

''No, no.'' Madame Xavier frowned. ''That's not what I mean. Something is missing in your sex life.''

''Well,'' Sarah supplied. ''That's no mystery. Jill

and Randy have a second virginity pact. No nooky until the wedding night.''

The entire group laughed. Jill blushed.

Madame Xavier shook her head. "No. That's not what I'm talking about." The older woman stared deeply into Jill's eyes. "But you know what I mean."

"Yes," Jill said, and nervously brought two fingers to her lips.

"You must fill in the blanks," Madame Xavier told her, "if you want the marriage to succeed."

Jill nodded and ducked her head. Eden had the strangest suspicion the young woman was struggling hard not to cry. Her own chest knotted up and she wondered what was going on.

"Now you. Drink up." Madame Xavier pointed a finger at Eden.

"No, that's all right. I'm not playing."

"Drink up." Madame Xavier sank her hands on her hips and glowered.

"Go ahead, Eden," Jill whispered to her. "It's just a game."

Eden realized that all eyes in the room were staring at her. Not wanting to be the odd woman out, she swallowed the tepid tea and presented her leaves to the fortune-teller.

"Ah," Madame Xavier smiled. "Lots of sexual adventure in your future. You're a brave girl. You've taken the first step. It will pay off for you. Games and fun and much, much pleasure."

Everyone tittered.

"But beware," Madame Xavier admonished.

"Beware?" Eden repeated, a shiver pressing against her spine.

"Your plans may backfire if you're not careful." Madame Xavier's eyes darkened knowingly. "Remember, you cannot cage the wind."

Uneasiness pierced her skin. "I don't understand. What does that mean?"

Madame Xavier didn't answer her. She had already gone on to read the next woman's tea leaves.

But Eden didn't really need a response to her question. She knew Alec was the wind of which the woman spoke. And she didn't want to cage him. Honestly. And yet, she couldn't shake the vaguely queasy sensation rolling through her at the tea-leaf reader's remarks.

After the fortunes were all told and everyone had a good laugh, they moved on to the gifts. When Jill opened Eden's gift basket and slowly drew out the contents, everyone applauded.

"Eden's baskets are inspired," Sarah said.

You have no idea, Eden thought.

Jill's eyes met Eden's. "How did you know?" she whispered. "My secret?"

Eden wasn't quite certain what Jill was talking about but she assumed she was referring to the playboy and the virgin fantasy. "Alec was a big help in coming up with the idea."

Jill returned everything to the silver champagne bucket that served as the container for the racy theme. "Thank you."

"It's Alec's gift to you and Randy, not mine."

"But you're the creator. It's very special."

"I'm happy you're pleased."

By the time Jill finished opening the packages, Eden was antsy to leave. She was supposed to meet Alec at the Grand Duchess at seven and it was already five-thirty. She didn't have much time to get back to the city.

Just then the back door opened and the sound of masculine voices filled the house. And then the guys appeared in the doorway. Zach, Alec and a tall, strapping man Eden hadn't met.

"Great timing," Sarah said. "We were about to have refreshments. Why don't you join us, fellas?"

"Can't," Alec said, looking at his watch. "I have an appointment in the city and I can't be late."

The big guy moved across the room to sweep Jill into his arms and planted a hot, passionate kiss on her lips. Eden pegged him for her fiancé, Randy.

"Missed you, babe. How's the party?" He murmured to Jill.

But Eden's gaze was glued to Alec.

He was dressed in a faded basketball jersey and a pair of holey gray sweat shorts that molded to his muscular butt and showed off his long, lean, athletic legs.

He had an orange basketball tucked under one arm and he rested one shoulder against the doorjamb, while gazing out over the women like a sultan surveying his harem.

Eden squinted against the shaft of late afternoon sunlight slanting through the window behind him and bathing him in a bright wash of yellow light. His insouciant, rebel's slouch and sultry half-lidded eyes belied the steadfastness of his strong chin, the reliable promise of his chiseled cheekbones.

The contrast between his looks and his attitude was striking. A wolf in sheep's clothing. A Greek god gone wrong. A cherubic choirboy with a deep-seated penchant for sin.

When one of the women hopped up from her seat and rushed over to sling an arm around his neck, a blind rush of possessiveness raised the hairs on her arms and had Eden fighting off a barrage of strange emotions.

This was exactly the reason she hadn't wanted to meet his friends and family. Getting to know him outside of the restricted perimeters of the Grand Duchess was not part of her game plan.

He hadn't yet spied her tucked away in the corner beside the draperies. Eden's gut fisted. What would he think about her being here? She'd violated one of her own rules and she had no excuse for it. She wished she could melt into the furniture.

Then he glanced across the room and spotted her.

A sexy, lopsided grin lifted one corner of his mouth and leisurely progressed to the other side, charming away her doubts and fears. Eden's heart swelled with a fresh tumble of new emotions.

No denying the sultry blaze in his hot eyes.

He was happy to see her.

8

ALEC COULDN'T BELIEVE his eyes. Eden, his fantasy goddess, was right there in his sister's living room, breaking her stipulations.

For some reason, he found the idea of her violating her own rules sexy as hell.

She smiled as he approached. A sly, seductive smile that took his breath away and made him think of throwing her over his shoulder caveman-style and carting her off to the nearest bedroom. Never mind his mother and four sisters being in the vicinity.

He raked his gaze over her.

She wore a long black coat, which shouldn't have been provocative, but combined with those black leather vixen boots wrapped around her legs, it was. In fact, his mind splintered off in a million directions as he pondered exactly what that coat cloaked.

Her chestnut curls were pinned loosely to her head and long, soft tendrils trailed around her heart-shaped face. He imagined himself reaching over, removing the pins and watching the rest of her hair tumble down.

Small pearl earrings and a pearl choker shone with a luminescent glow in the light from the nearby window. He was close enough to spot a hint of sheer black lace peeping from the V-neck of her collar.

What was she wearing under that coat? He had to find out. His throat tightened.

"Why hello," he said, surprised to find he could even speak. "What are you doing here?"

"My assistant called in sick. So I brought the basket over myself. I'm afraid your sister took me hostage and wouldn't let me leave." Eden shrugged.

She appeared serenely nonchalant and she might have gotten away with her act if he hadn't caught the movement of her fingering something clutched in her palm. When he recognized the worry stone, he had to force himself not to grin. No matter how cool she tried to play it, the woman was as unsettled by the potent sexual energy surging between them as he was.

"That's our Sarah."

"She's quite persuasive."

"Sometimes to the point of being annoying. At other times, like now, I thank heavens for her steamroller personality."

"I was just about to leave." Eden gestured toward the front door.

"To keep your date with me."

She met his gaze and didn't flinch. "Yes."

He spread his arms wide. "Here I am."

"So I see."

"Who are you tonight?" he whispered, his blood racing in anticipation.

"I don't know. My plans have been thrown."

"We can adapt."

"Stop staring at me like that."

"Like what?"

"Like…you know." She fidgeted in her seat. "We don't want your family figuring out what's going on."

"Alec, Eden, we're going into the buffet. You guys up for some chow?" Sarah called as the rest of the guests filed into the dining room.

Eden got to her feet. "Thank you so much, Sarah, it's been very nice meeting you all, but I really do have to get back to the city."

"I'll give you a ride," Alec volunteered. He liked the idea of having her in his car. That way she couldn't run away from him until he was ready to let her go.

"That's okay," Eden said pointedly, and shot him a dirty look. Apparently, she didn't like it when she wasn't in control. "I'll call a taxi."

"Why would you do that when you could ride in a Ferrari?"

"You keep a car in the city?"

"An indulgence."

"But a Ferrari?" She blinked.

He shrugged. "A cliché perhaps, but it suits my *Single Guy* image."

"Let him give you a lift," Sarah encouraged. "The Ferrari is a convertible. Believe me, you'll get the thrill of your life."

His sister had no idea just how weighted her words were. At the thought of Eden's dark hair whipping around her face, her head thrown back to catch the wind, a sigh of ecstasy on her lips, Alec felt himself harden. He had to get them both out of here, pronto.

"Okay," Eden said. "If you're sure it's no trouble."

"No trouble at all," he assured her, his hands itching to shove themselves up under her coat and see what goodies lay beyond.

Eden sat beside Alec, her heart revving higher than the Ferrari's engine. He seemed as restless as she as he drummed his fingers against the steering wheel and stared intently out at the road.

Surreptitiously, she observed him, peeking at him through slightly lowered lashes. He was absolutely gorgeous even in his ratty basketball clothes. She spied the sexy shadow of whiskers along his jaw and she ached to run her palm over the bristly surface, Masculine power radiated from him. He was so damned alive. Eden couldn't help smiling as her mind spun into sinful territory.

"What are you thinking about that has you grinning that smug little grin?" he asked.

"Hmm." She sounded pleased that she'd bewitched him. "Wouldn't you like to know?"

"Very much."

With a provocative wink, she moistened her lips and then began unbuttoning her coat.

"What are you doing?" he croaked.

"I'm hot."

"Yes, babe, you most certainly are." He almost ran a red light, the yellow switching to crimson just as the Ferrari slipped beneath the traffic signal.

"Keep your eyes on the road," she instructed.

"Yes, ma'am." He twisted the rearview mirror around so that he could watch her. He had a feeling she was up to no good, and he loved the expectancy of some outlandish action.

Blood, heated and languid, pooled in his groin. Every nerve ending in his blood leaped and jumped with electrical excitement.

Eden made nimble work of the buttons. Slowly, she spread her legs just a few inches. The duster fell open, exposing an expanse of her silky black body stocking. His sharp gasp of approval was her reward and gave her permission to push her own limits a little further.

"You're not wearing a bra," he said huskily, "and that teeny black skirt is driving me insane. I hope you realize that."

"Mmm." She trailed a hand from her breasts to her stomach to her thighs and angled him a sultry look.

"Have mercy, woman. This is unmitigated torture. I love how you can go from cautious worrywart to bedazzling hedonist. This naughty versus nice thing you have going on is driving me nuts."

Eden looked down at his lap. His rock-hard erection a testament to what he was saying. "Oh, the torture is just starting."

She unpinned her hair, tossed her head and watched him watch her curls cascade to her shoulders. Moistening her bottom lip with her tongue, she unfastened her seatbelt. Eden raised two fingers to her mouth,

damped them with her saliva, then tucked them between her legs and up under the hem of her skirt.

Alec's indrawn breath echoed in the car and beads
of perspiration instantly formed on his upper lip.
"Are you doing what I think you're doing?"

Yes, she was daring to pleasure herself. Right there
in his car, in the waning daylight, with traffic whizzing by.

Alec braked suddenly, pulled off the road and
turned the car around.

"What are you doing?" she whispered.

"I'm not letting you have fun all by yourself," he
muttered with determination.

"Where are you taking me?"

"Make-out Point."

"Let me guess, your old high-school days."

"Uh-huh."

"You take a lot of girls there?"

"Just the naughty ones."

"So," she said as she thought of a new game,
"you're the captain of the basketball team."

She took her fingers, the very same fingers that just
minutes before had been stroking her warm moistness
and rubbed them over his basketball jersey in a bold
gesture designed to arouse them both.

"Yeah," he said. "And you're new at Glenville
High."

"Uh-huh."

"Are you going to try out for the cheerleading
squad?" he asked, guiding the Ferrari along the tree-
lined road.

"I'm not that kind of a girl." She purred and ran her fingers down his stomach to stroke his erection stretching out his old gray gym shorts. "Imagine how I would shock the fans when I asked them to give me an F and then a U and then a…"

"I see your point," he said, pulling to a stop in a copse of trees off the side of the one-lane road, overlooking the lake.

Eden turned to him, her heart hammering at an alarming rate. She loved how this game had just evolved, unplanned and unscripted. The mental connection they shared when it came to sex was simply unbelievable and highly erotic.

Secretly, she'd always dreamed of a lover who'd play such tantalizing games with her. A lover who understood the importance of imagination in heightening the sexual response. It seemed as if all her forbidden fantasies were on the verge of coming true. She was about to put all the rehearsal she'd had preparing sexy gift baskets to practical use.

Making out with Alec in the front seat of an incredible sports car could only enhance her creativity. And her femininity.

And, because of the slinky cat-suit that covered most of her body, save for the slit cut out at a crucial spot, she didn't have to worry about unveiling her burn scars tonight.

"Do you promise not to speak of this tomorrow in the locker room?" she whispered huskily.

The air was thick with the smell of autumn and if

it weren't for their combined body heat, she might have been cold.

"A gentleman never kisses and tells."

"I have a ten-o'clock curfew. My father gets really mad when I'm late. I'd hate to get grounded," she said, playing the game.

"I'll be finished with you in plenty of time."

He slid his seat back as far as it would go and then reached for her, dragging her over the gearshift and into his lap.

"Oh my," she whispered.

The steering wheel was flush against the left side of her rib cage, his erection a lance of solid steel tucked beneath her bottom.

When he looked at her that way she felt as if she were the sexiest woman on the planet. She caught the fever of his sexual radiance, inhaled sharply as it expanded inside her.

He smelled of autumn and leather and just plain Alec. He took her right arm, wrapped it around his neck and then he was kissing her.

His lips caressed hers at an upward angle since she was positioned above him. The smooth glide of his tongue was faultless, neither too hesitant nor too demanding.

In fact it was a stupendous kiss, perfectly performed with just the right amount of pressure, moisture and sexy sound.

The kiss soothed her nerves and vanquished any lingering qualms she might have about seeing this thing through in an open convertible parked by the waterside. The wind was a cool balm against her heated skin, their combined fragrance an aroma of sweet pleasure.

Their tongues dueled. First, he was the conqueror and then she, until finally he won as his mouth muddled her senses. Arousal scissored into a brilliant haze of estrogen, testosterone and adrenaline.

She closed her eyes and drifted away on a cloud of pure contentment. He kissed her as if he knew and understood every single thought that crossed her mind. Shamelessly she arched into his body and whimpered for much more than mere kisses.

Pushing aside the lapel of her duster, he lightly pinched one of her straining nipples between a thumb and forefinger, sending skillful darts of pleasure shooting through her aching breast. This felt so good, so right, so perfect.

"Yes, yes," she groaned. "This is exactly what I want." She needed this, needed him on so many levels.

"Talk to me, sweetheart. Tell me everything."

"You have the most gorgeous cock," Eden dared, letting herself go and gleefully assuming the role of class slut screwing the captain of the basketball team. It was incredibly exciting and liberating, beyond her wildest dreams. "I want to feel you inside me. Now."

She couldn't believe she'd ever felt this way. Her body ached, her womanhood throbbed ripe and juicy and ready for him. She loved this. Loved driving him mad with desire. Loved seeing the expression of awe on his face. She, of the burn scars and unlived fantasies, was sending this experienced, worldly playboy into the stratosphere.

Egged on by her thoughts, she panted with excitement, wriggled with abandon, groaned with escalating tension.

He stopped kissing her and she opened her eyes. His face was so close to hers, his gaze intense, sharp and hungry. The weight of his palm on her thigh had Eden catching her breath.

"How do you get this thing off?" he murmured, stroking the scoop neck of her body stocking.

"You don't."

"Then how...?"

She leaned in close to his ear. "Crotchless," she whispered.

He literally shuddered and dipped his head. He slid his mouth over her chin, down her neck to the smooth hollow of her throat. His tongue strummed her skin while his hair tickled the underside of her jaw.

His touch affected everything. The tickling made her squirm. The brush of his lips swept a burning itch over her collarbone. The steady vibration of his beating heart shook her bones. The bend of her elbows grew damp with desire. The back of her knees weakened and between her legs she was hot and wet and starving for attention.

She moaned softly and arched against him. "Hurry, stud. My curfew, remember. My old man will ground me for a week if I'm late."

"You won't be late."

"Promise."

"I'll have you home in time."

"Then you better get busy."

"Hold on a minute," he said shakily. "My seat belt is still buckled."

She hadn't even noticed the poke of cool metal in her side. She was too caught up in the magic. She moved away from him, rolling back into her seat while he fumbled with the belt.

Her body pulsed and burned, alive with need and desire.

"Hurry," she urged again. "Hurry."

Before I lose my courage. Before I start thinking about worst-case scenarios.

Don't think. Don't think. Just feel.

Gritting her teeth, she followed her own advice, focusing on her body's response to the mad, ravaging rush of sensation.

She thought she would split right into two pieces, so desperate was the heaviness blooming within her groin. Along with undoing the seat belt, Alec stopped to free his penis, unsheathing the proud, large erection from the button fly of his gym shorts.

"Condom?" she asked, barely able to speak against the riptide of heat blasting through her veins.

"Glove compartment."

Frantically she yanked open the glove compartment and searched for the condom. She was about to cry out in despair when she found the small foil packet. She let out a sigh of relief.

He fumbled with the packet and even dropped it

Play the
"LAS VEGAS"
GAME

TURN THE PAGE TO PLAY! **Details inside!**

Play the

"LAS VEGAS" Game

and get

3 FREE GIFTS!

FREE GIFTS!

FREE GIFTS!

1. Pull back all 3 tabs on the card at right. Then check the claim chart to see what we have for you — 2 FREE BOOKS and a gift — ALL YOURS! ALL FREE!

2. Send back this card and you'll receive brand-new Harlequin® Blaze™ novels. These books have a cover price of $4.50 each in the U.S. and $5.25 each in Canada, but they are yours to keep absolutely free.

3. There's no catch. You're under no obligation to buy anything. We charge nothing — ZERO — for your first shipment. And you don't have to make any minimum number of purchases — not even one!

4. The fact is, thousands of readers enjoy receiving their books by mail from the Harlequin Reader Service®. They enjoy the convenience of home delivery...they like getting the best new novels at discount prices, BEFORE they're available in stores...and they love their *Heart to Heart* newsletter featuring author news, horoscopes, recipes, book reviews and much more!

5. We hope that after receiving your free books you'll want to remain a subscriber. But the choice is yours — to continue or cancel, any time at all! So why not take us up on our invitation, with no risk of any kind. You'll be glad you did!

Visit us online at
www.eHarlequin.com

FREE!
No Obligation to Buy!
No Purchase Necessary!

Play the

"LAS VEGAS" Game

PEEL BACK HERE ▶
PEEL BACK HERE ▶
PEEL BACK HERE ▶

YES! I have pulled back the 3 tabs. Please send me all the free Harlequin® Blaze™ books and the gift for which I qualify. I understand that I am under no obligation to purchase any books, as explained on the back and opposite page.

350 HDL DNYQ   150 HDL DQD6

FIRST NAME	LAST NAME

ADDRESS

APT.#	CITY

STATE/PROV.   ZIP/POSTAL CODE   (H-B-09/02)

7 7 7	**GET 2 FREE BOOKS & A FREE MYSTERY GIFT!**
🍀 🍀 🍀	**GET 2 FREE BOOKS!**
🍒 🍒 🍒	**GET 1 FREE BOOK!**
🔔 🔔 🔔	**TRY AGAIN!**

The Harlequin Reader Service® — Here's how it works:

Accepting your 2 free books and gift places you under no obligation to buy anything. You may keep the books and gift and return the shipping statement marked "cancel." If you do not cancel, about a month later we'll send you 4 additional novels and bill you just $3.80 each in the U.S., or $4.21 each in Canada, plus 25¢ shipping & handling per book and applicable taxes if any.* That's the complete price and — compared to cover prices of $4.50 each in the U.S. and $5.25 each in Canada — it's quite a bargain! You may cancel at any time, but if you choose to continue, every month we'll send you 4 more books, which you may either purchase at the discount price or return to us and cancel your subscription.

*Terms and prices subject to change without notice. Sales tax applicable in N.Y. Canadian residents will be charged applicable provincial taxes and GST.

BUSINESS REPLY MAIL
FIRST-CLASS MAIL   PERMIT NO. 717-003   BUFFALO, NY

POSTAGE WILL BE PAID BY ADDRESSEE

HARLEQUIN READER SERVICE
3010 WALDEN AVE
PO BOX 1867
BUFFALO NY 14240-9952

NO POSTAGE
NECESSARY
IF MAILED
IN THE
UNITED STATES

once before successfully getting it opened and the rubber rolled into place.

"Come here, vixen," he growled, and pulled her back into his lap.

This time, she straddled him, her knees digging into the plush leather seat on either side of his thick, masculine thighs.

She pushed her hands up under his basketball jersey, anxious to feel his muscled chest beneath her splayed palms and cuddled his neck.

They kissed, harder this time with sharp nips and hungry nibbles instead of soft strokes and gentle caresses. Then when he broke the kiss to suckle one of her nipples through the material of her body stocking, she just about came undone.

His throbbing penis was behind her, pressed flush against her bottom and straining hard for his share of the action. If she didn't have him soon, she was going to go absolutely mad.

He sucked harder at her nipple, his hands wrapped tightly around her waist. She threw back her head, arched her back and accidentally honked the car horn.

Neither one of them noticed or cared. They were lost. Swept away on a tide of carnal lust.

She was slick and wet. With one hand he felt for the opening in the body stocking. For one precarious moment, she froze, wondering if he might feel the scar or if his entry into that seldom-used place might hurt her.

But in the fading light, between their clothing, his fingers were desensitized to nuances of her flawed skin. And when he lifted her up and eased her onto his shaft, she slid right down with surprising ease.

A perfect match. A perfect fit.

It didn't hurt a bit. In fact, the sensitive rubbing was quite erotic.

Finally, finally, she was putting all her esoteric knowledge to good use.

He bucked his hips driving himself hard into her. His desperate fury was at once startling and liberating. They were wild as two beasts, blinded by passion.

She clawed at his shoulders. He tugged on her hair. She pressed her forehead flat against his and stared down into his eyes.

Alec kissed her as he was making love to her. She surrendered to the rhythm, to the friction. They sparked off each other. She eagerly parried his thrusts.

It seemed his hands and lips were everywhere. Her eyelids, her cheek, the curve of her spine. Eden's blood pounded, swelling in her temples like the crescendo of a classical symphony—Alec, Alec, Alec.

Harder, faster, deeper he penetrated, rocking himself up into her.

Yes. Yes. She was close. So very close to having her first orgasm with a partner. It was sublime. It was primitive. It was all-encompassing, this intimate union of two bodies.

"Eden," he gasped in a strangled voice. "I'm coming. I'm sorry...I don't..."

The tide of his orgasm snatched the words from his mouth. He shuddered into her and gave a rough, masculine cry. Even though she lost her own climax, the fact that she'd reduced him to such an elemental state filled her with an earthy contentment. She stayed astride him, felt his erection diminish.

His head slipped back against the seat. His hands, which had been holding her in place over his erection, relaxed. His eyes shuttered closed and his breathing escaped in tight, air-hungry gasps.

Then he reached up a hand, cupped the back of her head in his palm and brought her face down to his.

He kissed her. Softly, sweetly, with deep appreciation and a rapt sense of wonder.

"That was absolutely incredible," he murmured against her mouth. "Thank you."

"You're welcome," she said, suddenly feeling shy now that the intensity was waning.

"I'm sorry I came too soon for you, but give me a few minutes to recover and we'll try again."

"Okay."

They gazed into each other's eyes.

"I need to move," she whispered. "I'm getting a cramp in my leg."

"All right."

She slid off him, rolled over the gearshift and collapsed into the passenger seat. She readjusted her clothes while he dealt with the aftermath of their lovemaking.

"If you want," he said, his eyes soft with a sated gleam. "I can take care of you right now." He inched a hand toward the hem of her skirt.

"Uh, it's okay." Swiftly she crossed her legs, warding off his hand.

It was a little late to get panicky, but when she thought of his fingers skimming her down there, without the pressure of his own desire distracting him, she feared he would indeed feel her scars.

You have to let him see them sometime, Eden. If this whole affair is going to be a success.

Not now. Not yet. She wasn't ready to reveal her vulnerability. Especially here in a sports car beside the lake.

But before she had time to come up with an excuse for why she didn't want him to finger her to orgasm, the blast from a police car siren and the strobe of red and blue lights had them both jumping.

"Holy crap," Eden said. "Busted. My old man's gonna have a fit."

Alec grinned over at her. "Still playing the game."

Yes. Playing the game gave her back the sense of control that had scattered into fear when he had reached for her most private place.

"Well, well, well," the burly middle-aged trooper said as he strolled over to the driver's side of the Ferrari, clipboard in hand. "If it isn't Alec Ramsey, up to his old tricks."

9

DREAMILY, ALEC GAZED out the window of his office, his mind stuck on Eden. No matter how hard he tried to focus on work, he couldn't pry his thoughts off Saturday night and the free-for-all in the front seat of his Ferrari.

Or the way he'd let her down again.

Alec cringed. What was the matter with him? No woman had ever pushed him beyond the limits of his control. He hadn't satisfied her and he felt like a greedy failure. Getting his climax while leaving her hanging. If the police officer hadn't shown up when he did, Alec would have made certain Eden had an orgasm.

She had readily forgiven him for coming too quickly, but he couldn't forgive or excuse himself. When he'd dropped her off at Wickedly Wonderful, as she insisted, Eden had leaned down and whispered in his ear, "Be prepared for Tuesday night, mister, because I'm going to rock your world."

As if she hadn't already.

Alec propped his elbows on his desk and sank his chin into his upturned palms.

It sounded clichéd, but honestly he had never met

a woman like Eden. He recalled every little thing about her. The velvet of her skin, the rasp of her moans, the gentle curve of her neck, the spark of passion in her eyes, the rich, earthy scent of her arousal.

And no one had ever responded to his touch in quite the same way she did. Magically she dissolved into satin at the slightest brush of his hand. Alluringly she unfurled like a rose when his tongue grazed her lips. Temptingly she surrendered all restraint when his body joined hers.

Her appetites matched his own, a rarefied trait, indeed. Her life force was a thing of heart-stopping beauty.

She was luminescent in her womanly glow and powerful in her innate sexuality. She made him feel like the sexiest creature on the face of the earth.

And he had gone and spoiled it all by losing self-control.

Dammit!

Alec slammed a fist on his desk. Even though his premature climax was a compliment to her skill and desirability, he couldn't believe he'd been unable to forgo his own pleasure for the sake of hers.

He was a selfish, greedy jerk and he was appalled at his behavior. He based his reputation on treating women right. In the pages of his magazine, he extolled the virtues of extended foreplay and making sure your partner was sated before taking your own release.

He'd never had a problem like this. He was ashamed of himself and determined to rectify the situation. Tomorrow night was going to be all about her. Whatever she wanted, he would give it to her. He would be her sex slave and she his goddess. No arguments allowed.

Agitatedly he tapped his foot against the leg of his desk and plowed his hands through his hair. He was so lost in thought that at first he didn't hear Randy come into his office.

It wasn't until his best friend plopped down on the leather love seat and heaved a deep sigh that Alec looked up.

"Hey, man. You look awful."

"I feel worse."

"You sick? If you're sick, stay away from me." Alec raised his palms to ward off any unpleasant germs Randy might be harboring. "I'm seeing Eden tomorrow night and I want to be in tip-top shape."

Randy pulled a hand down his face and shook his head. "It's Jill."

"Is she sick?"

"She's called off the wedding." Randy's voice cracked and there was no mistaking the sound of unshed tears.

That brittle, heartbreaking noise brought Alec up short. He'd never seen his friend melt down emotionally. Not even when he'd broken his ankle skydiving. Not even when Randy had been forced to put his fourteen-year-old Labrador retriever to sleep.

Alec got up from his desk and walked over to sit beside him on the love seat. He lightly punched his shoulder to comfort his distraught buddy the only way he knew how. They sat there staring morosely at each other for a long moment.

"What happened?" Alec finally ventured.

He'd never been crazy about the idea of Randy's impending marriage, but seeing his friend looking so torn up knifed him hard in the gut.

"I don't know. All Jill said was that she thought maybe we needed to take a breather and reevaluate our relationship. She doesn't want to see me or talk to me for at least two weeks. What the hell does this mean?" Randy shot him a baleful glance.

Helplessly Alec shook his head. "Women, who can figure 'em."

"Do you think she's cheating on me?"

"Of course not," Alec lied smoothly. He didn't know whether Jill was being faithful or not but he didn't want to inject doubt into Randy's mind.

"I love her, man. I mean serious, stone cold love her. It's ripping my heart out that she won't even discuss the problem with me. I guess I'm just a typical, clueless guy, because I didn't even know there was a problem. I thought everything was fine between us. We have fun. We stay up late just shooting the breeze about anything and everything." Randy paused. "Or at least we did."

"When did all this happen?"

"Saturday night. After we left the wedding shower."

"How long of a postponement is she talking?"

"Indefinitely."

Alec grunted and rose to his feet. It certainly didn't

sound good. To think Randy had waited twenty-eight years to find his true love and now this. It made no sense. He didn't understand. His heart gave a strange jerk of disappointment.

If something like this could happen to a happy, stable couple like Randy and Jill, what hope is there for the rest of us?

Alec shoved his hands in his pockets. This was exactly why he avoided permanent relationships—too much opportunity for heartache.

"I'm losing her and I don't even know what I've done wrong."

"You'll work it out."

Randy shook his head. "I'm beginning to think you and your uncle Mac were right all along. Marriage— the ties that bind and gag."

"We weren't right. Love and marriage are the underpinnings of our society."

What? Where in the hell had that come from? Of course marriage was a ball and chain around your neck. Love ensnared you in a stranglehold and sucked the life right out of you. Hadn't he witnessed his father's slow descent? Hadn't he enjoyed the delicious fruits of singledom for a blissful twenty-seven years? Hadn't bachelorhood provided him with an excellent way to make a living?

Why tempt fate? Why mess with perfection? Why fix it if it ain't broke?

His life was good. Very good.

So why did he suddenly feel antsy and claustrophobic? Why did he have a strong desire to go dive off a cliff with a parachute just to prove he was alive and kicking and decidedly unattached?

You're just trying to make Randy feel better. Being a good friend, he assured himself. *Don't panic.*

Alec clamped Randy on the shoulder. "Obviously Jill's just got cold feet. She loves you. I've never doubted that about her."

"Really?" Randy looked hopeful. "You honestly think so?"

"Sure." Alec nodded. "You guys will work this out. Count on it. Just give her a little breathing room."

"Thanks." Randy managed a small smile. "You're probably right."

Alec forced a smile of his own. For his friend's sake, he prayed it was true.

THE WIND CHIMES over the door tinkled and Eden glanced up to see Jill Fincher standing hesitantly at the threshold of Wickedly Wonderful. Her eyes widened as she gazed around the room, taking it all in.

"Jill, hello." Eden put down the staple gun she'd been wielding in the process of creating a new basket she'd dubbed the Thrill of the Chase, and she was in the middle of bringing her edgy fantasies to fruition.

"Hi," Jill said shyly.

"Come on in." Eden moved from around the counter to motion the other woman on into the store.

"Is this a bad time?" Jill gnawed her lips and gestured at the door with a hand. "Because if this is a bad time, I can come back later."

"Nonsense. I'm at your disposal. What can I do for you?"

Jill took a deep breath and eyed a large vibrator on a shelf at chin level. "Um...er..." She moistened her lips. "This is sort of difficult for me to ask."

"Whatever you tell me will go no further," Eden promised.

Jill blew out her held breath. "Here's the deal. I'd like you to teach me how to be sexy."

"What?"

Jill looked so earnest that Eden almost broke into laughter. Good thing Ashley was off on a delivery. She would have been rolling on the floor laughing her butt off at the notion of Eden teaching someone how to be sexy.

Don't put yourself down. Saturday night was the sexiest thing that ever happened to you.

Okay. True. She was on the road to becoming sexier.

"Please. I really, really need your help. One look at the basket you created for my...my honeymoon..." Jill hiccuped and then burst into tears.

"What is it? What's wrong? Did you totally hate the basket?"

"No!" Jill wailed. "That's the problem. I loved it."

"So why are you crying? I didn't mean to make you cry."

"Eden, it was uncanny how you seemed to have captured the essence of my relationship with Randy, and you don't even know me. And then when that tea-leaf reader said something was missing in my life…'' She broke off again, overcome with emotion.

"Come." Eden took Jill's hand and guided her to the back of the store. She pulled out a chair from the table. "Sit."

Jill sat.

Eden went to the little fridge she kept stocked with beverages and took out a soft drink. She popped the top and passed it to the tearful woman. "Have something cold to drink, calm down and then you can explain what this is all about."

Nodding, Jill sipped her soda for a few minutes while Eden sat opposite her and waited patiently. She was flattered that Jill had come seeking advice, but she had no idea what had upset her so.

"I called off the wedding."

"What!"

"I told Randy I needed time off to think things through."

"Are you serious?"

"Deadly serious. I've been miserable for weeks, but the wedding shower pushed me over the edge."

"You can't take the tea-leaf reading seriously. It didn't mean a thing."

You can't cage the wind, the phrase Madame Xavier had spoken to her flitted through Eden's head. She was good at giving advice but not too hot at taking it. If she were being honest, she would admit she'd been upset by the tea-leaf reading, too.

"But Madame Xavier was right." Jill picked at a fuzz ball on her sweater. "Something *is* missing."

"Don't you love Randy?"

"Oh yes, very much."

"And he loves you?"

"I don't doubt his devotion for a moment."

"So what's the problem?"

Jill took a deep breath. "You heard Sarah say Randy and I were committed to a second virginity. We'd planned on waiting for our wedding night to have sex."

"Uh-huh."

"Well, that's not the whole truth."

Eden grinned. "You two have been having sex."

"No!" Jill's hand went to her throat. "I mean we've been playing around some, sure."

Images of how she and Alec had been playing around popped into her head and she had to struggle hard not to grin.

"But," Jill continued, "here's the thing. This isn't a second virginity for me. I actually *am* a virgin."

"What's so bad about that?"

"Randy doesn't know."

"So tell him."

"I can't."

"Why not?"

Jill kneaded her forehead with two fingers. "Randy's had so much experience with women, and here I am a twenty-six-year-old virgin. Won't he think something's wrong with me?"

"Why would he think that?"

"It's freakish, being a virgin in your middle twenties, but I was waiting until I found the right guy and fell in love. And then Randy wanted to do this second virginity thing to prove to me that his old playboy lifestyle was behind him.''

''But that's a good thing. It shows how serious he is about marriage.''

''I know, but now I'm feeling I haven't lived enough. That I need a few notches on my bedpost, too, so when I'm an old lady in a nursing home I don't think back and regret not having explored my sexuality a little more. I hate being so inexperienced.''

''You want to sleep with someone other than your fiancé?'' Eden stared at her.

''Yes. No. I don't know.'' Jill dropped her face into her hands. ''I'm so confused.''

''I can see how the Playboy and the Virgin basket might have hit a sour note, but don't let your doubts destroy a great relationship.''

''No, no. Quite the opposite. The basket is what made me certain that you were the one who could help me.''

''I really don't understand.''

''Oh, Eden, I'm so scared I'll be a disappointment to Randy. He's accustomed to sexually sophisticated women with lots of naughty boudoir tricks up their sleeves. Accomplished women who know exactly how to please a man. Women like you.''

''Yeah, that's me all right.'' Eden snorted indelicately. ''Sophisticated, sexy and accomplished.''

''It is!''

''If you only knew how little experience I've had you'd laugh at the irony of your request.''

Jill's eyes rounded. ''But you create those erotic baskets.''

''Fantasy. All fantasy.''

''Not according to Alec.''

''Alec has been talking about me? About us?''

A cold hand of disappointment gripped her spine. How could he tell tales out of the bedroom to his friends? Especially after he had promised to keep their affair quiet. Distress had her clenching her jaw. She had trusted him and he'd betrayed her by spreading locker-room stories.

''Oh, no,'' Jill denied. ''Alec hasn't said anything. Randy is the one who told me Alec met a real sex kitten who was giving him a run for his money in the bedroom.''

''Alec must have said something for your fiancé to draw that conclusion.''

Jill sighed. ''And Randy sounded kind of wistful when he said 'sex kitten.' Like I *wasn't* a sex kitten and he was missing out on something.''

''You're probably imagining things or at least blowing it out of proportion.''

''Anyway, I just assumed it was you.'' Jill cringed. ''You *are* the sex kitten Alec's been sleeping with, aren't you?''

Alec had bragged to Randy about his sex kitten. Eden was disgruntled that he had blabbed, even if he'd kept her name anonymous, but a small part of her was pleased to think he considered her worthy of the "sex kitten" moniker. "I suppose I am."

Unless he had another woman waiting in the wings she knew nothing about. Ouch.

"Please, Eden, help me save my relationship with Randy. Teach me."

Jayne had taught Eden and now Eden was about to teach Jill. They created a chain. Adventuresome women sharing their sex secrets and empowering their sisters to greater orgasmic heights.

"Jill," she said. "I'd be honored to show you every sex trick I know."

THE NEXT EVENING, Eden arrived at the Grand Duchess armed for *bear*. She had an hourglass tucked under one arm, and a CD player with a recording of "Sixty-Minute Man" in the other.

The premature orgasms stopped here and now. Around her shoulder she carried a satchel chock-full of surprises for the secret-spilling Mr. Alec Ramsey.

Eden was still a little angry with him for telling Randy about their bedroom high jinks, but not too mad to spoil the night. In fact, she was going to use it as a bargaining chip against him, upping the ante.

She'd show him sex kitten.

Sex panther was more like it.

Growling under her breath, she headed for the elevators.

She had splurged on a manicure, a pedicure and a facial. She'd shaved her legs, plucked her eyebrows and waxed her upper lip. She was smooth and pampered and sleekly groomed. Her hair was pulled back in a secure bun and she wore sensible flats.

Tonight she was an overworked Manhattan female CEO. in a black bustier with a garter and thigh-high stockings on underneath her staid gray business suit. An executive who liked tying men up and having her way with them.

And Alec would be her boy toy.

Tonight was about sweet revenge. She'd teach him to talk out of school.

By the time Alec knocked on the door, Eden had music playing, candles flickering and the champagne uncorked. When she opened the door, he bound inside like an enthusiastic hound dog on the scent of a raccoon. Before she could even say hello in the cool, calm executive voice she'd practiced all morning, Alec swept her into his arms and kissed her.

A frisson shot through her body and she sucked his bottom lip.

His sharp hiss of breath delighted her and she slipped from his lips to snack on his neck.

"God." He groaned. "I thought tonight would never get here. The waiting kills me."

"Ah," she said. "That's part of my plan."

"Your plan is more evil than world domination."

"Ha. You'll think evil when you find out what I have in store for you tonight."

He shuddered against her, pressed his lips to her ears and murmured, "Bring it on."

She laughed. "You say that now."

"Who are we tonight?"

"I run a multibillion-dollar company and you are the boy toy who sweeps the floor in my building."

"What's with the hourglass?" He eyed the hourglass on the dresser.

"My time is precious. I don't want to waste a minute, but I do want satisfaction. The hourglass will ensure proper foreplay."

"If I can last." He groaned. "I haven't been doing too well in that department and I want to apologize."

"The businesswoman accepts no excuses or apologies," she said coolly. "And you will last. My demands are always obeyed."

"Yes, ma'am." He grinned at her, his eyes glistening with dark passion.

She turned the hourglass over and the sand began to trickle through the slender neck.

"Remove your coat," she commanded and went to perch on the edge of the bed. Fascinated, Eden watched as Alec slowly slipped off his coat and then draped it over the doorknob.

"Pour us a glass of champagne." She waved a hand at the bucket.

He poured the champagne and gave her a glass. While warily eying each other, they sipped the dry, fruity liquid. She studied his lips as they closed over the glass. She couldn't tear her gaze away. He swallowed, his neck muscles smoothly working, his eyes never once leaving her face.

Unable to maintain the intensity of a prolonged stare, Eden lowered her eyelashes and drained her glass in three quick gulps. She needed a lightheadedness to get this scenario rolling. Jayne had assured her that, if she applied the techniques she'd taught her, Eden could indeed make Alec last a full hour.

She set the champagne flute on the bedside table and crooked a finger at him, her heart hammering at a furious pace. "Come here."

He came to her.

She sat on the bed, knees apart and he stood between her legs. "Sixty-Minute Man" was on a continuous loop and the song started over again, exalting the joyous qualities of a long-lasting lover.

"Strip," she demanded.

No kidding, he was so excited his fingers trembled when he reached for the buttons on his shirt. The simple knowledge that he was turned on, turned her on. He jerked at the shirt, desperate to get it off.

"No. Slower."

"You're killing me."

"Too bad."

With each button he undid, Eden felt herself grow moister, braver, hotter. When at last he took off the shirt, she reached for the waistband of his slacks and he rested his palms on her shoulders.

"Hands off. You can't touch me," she said. "Not until I say so."

He groaned again. "You wicked, wicked woman."

She leaned forward and kissed his navel. The dark hairs tickled her lips and when she boldly darted her tongue in and out of that small, dark tunnel, she saw that he had fisted his hands to keep from touching her.

"Good man."

After she tugged off his belt, she unzipped his pants. Slowly she eased his trousers and black boxer briefs down his hips.

His erection jutted out like a flagpole daring her to salute it.

"Kick off your shoes, peel off those socks and step out of your pants."

He complied. "Okay, when do I get to see you naked?"

"You don't."

"No." He shook his head. "No more of this one-sided stuff, Eden."

"Hush, boy toy, or I'll fire you."

"I'm not playing this game if you won't allow me to get you off."

Their gazes locked in a searing heat. She wondered what he was thinking. She wondered if he liked the game or not. Jayne had told her one of the most common masculine fantasies was to be tied up by a bossy woman. The dominatrix factor, Jayne called it. The fantasy was even more common, she'd explained, among powerful men.

And Alec was nothing if not powerful.

The tumescence building between them told Eden that yeah, Alec liked this game.

Now, for the coup de grâce. The item that would allow her, at long last, to get naked in front of him.

From the pocket of her gray wool business suit, Eden extracted a scarlet silk blindfold.

"Tie this over your eyes."

She held her breath, waiting to see if he would indeed play along.

"Yes, ma'am," he said, and she let out a sigh of relief as he did what she asked.

"Kneel down so I can check the bindings and make sure you've tied it tightly enough."

He went down on his knees, his head bowed, almost in her lap. A quick thrust of lust pushed through her veins as his hair grazed her skin.

Her fingers made sure the knots were tight. "Good work. Now on your feet."

He rose, his penis sideswiping her inner thigh on his way up. Eden had to clamp her lips together to suppress a moan.

"Get on the bed."

Blindly he reached out to feel for the covers and then he tumbled headlong onto the mattress.

"Spread-eagle," she said.

"What are you doing?"

"No questions."

She went to her satchel, removed the velvet ropes, then returned to the bed. The tension inside her mounted. Was she really brave enough to see this through?

She wrapped the ropes around her hand, experiencing the crush of velvet against her flesh.

"Do you trust me, Alec?"

"Not Alec," he said. "Boy toy."

"Do you trust me?"

"Yes."

"That's good," she said. "Because now it begins."

10

———

IT WAS AS IF she had peeked inside his brain and unearthed his favorite fantasy. How had Eden known he daydreamed about being tied up by a forceful woman?

But while light bondage was his secret kink, Alec had never experimented with it. He'd always been afraid that in spite of the thrill, he would panic at the loss of control. He was an active, dominant guy, and while being bound and blindfold stoked his desire, it also sent a worm of trepidation winnowing down his spine.

Should he protest? Should he tell her he'd changed his mind? Or should he simply surrender to the fantasy, let himself go, allow her to tie him up and have her way with him?

His skin tingled, alive with sensation, compensating for his lack of vision. His sense of smell sharpened and he inhaled her unique scent. Her deep-throated chuckle tickled his ears. He tasted his own nervousness, strong and slightly bitter, like over-brewed coffee.

"Have you considered," she said, while tying the

final rope around his left ankle, "that maybe I'm not trustworthy?"

How well did he know her really?

There, in the darkness, with his eyes covered and his limbs bound, a jolt of terrified delight gripped his body, mind and soul.

"What do you mean?" he whispered as a surge of testosterone bathed his brain and addled his senses. He was crazy for agreeing to this, but, man, what a crazy dream of insanity.

"What if I just went away and left you here?"

"But you wouldn't do that."

She said nothing.

He strained his ears, listening for the sound of her breathing. He felt her shimmy off the bed, her fingers lightly brushing his thighs.

"Eden?" He tried not to sound panicky. He wasn't panicking. She wouldn't leave him like this, naked and vulnerable, tied and revved up like a rocket aching for her finger to trip his trigger.

Would she?

He tested the bindings. They held.

"Eden."

Alec heard her feet pad across the carpet, then the unmistakable sound of the door opening and closing.

Oh crap, oh crap, oh crap. Don't go, baby, don't go!

Okay, this fantasy wasn't nearly as cool as it was in his imagination. He prayed she was still in the room and had only pretended to leave.

"Eden!" he bellowed, jerking against the ropes. "Get back here right now!"

A minute passed. Then two. Then three.

She wasn't coming back.

And then the door opened.

Alec inhaled sharply, his body tense—waiting.

She moved toward the bed, not speaking. He caught a whiff of her perfume. She smelled different now than she had before. Spicy and exotic.

The sound of a cracking whip broke the silence. He caught his breath.

What the hell had he gotten himself into? His chest squeezed and his erection flourished.

"I'm Mademoiselle Lizette," Eden said, in imitation of a thick French accent.

Leather tassels traced his cheek. Alec panted and arched his back. Damn, but she was extraordinary.

"If you are a good boy, I will not hurt you."

"Yes, Lizette."

She got onto the bed and straddled him. She squeezed him tightly with her stocking-covered thighs. When she leaned forward across his chest, he felt the sensuous glide of material against his nipples and realized she was wearing a bustier. A lace-gloved finger skimmed his armpit.

He hadn't known it was possible to get any harder, but his penis was so stiff he could have pummeled holes in Sheetrock.

And when she lightly, sweetly, feathered short, wet kisses over his nose, he collapsed into a vortex of sensory overload.

His fingers ached to touch her. His eyes yearned to see her. She'd robbed him of his vision and the use of his hands and feet, but she couldn't take away his sense of taste.

When she kissed his lips, he inhaled her, sucking her tongue into his mouth and stroking her with his own tongue in sinfully sensuous ways. His nose filled with the smell of her and he zoomed off on a speedway of sensation.

Intense!

After he finally let her go, she moved her mouth from his and went exploring. Like an intrepid world traveler, she took complete stock of his body.

She plunged her tongue into his ear and his groin caught fire. She sucked and licked and blew on his earlobe. She moved down and around to the crease under his chin. She pressed her lips against his Adam's apple and hummed a popular but naughty hip-hop ditty about women with big butts.

The ticklish vibrations encompassed his neck. She munched on the tendons extending from his ears to his shoulders and his penis tingled, crying out for equal time.

"Woman," he growled, "do you have any earthly idea what you're doing to me?"

"Hmm," she said, "your compass is pointing due North. I take that as a good sign."

"A very good sign. My compass is very happy to see you."

"Well, your compass is going to have to wait his turn."

Alec groaned.

"Patience is its own reward."

"To hell with that."

She laughed. "I'm working my way down. He'll get his due."

"He wants to give you *your* due."

"All in good time."

"You're a bewitching minx, Lizette."

"Just wait. We're only getting started."

She lived up to her promise and then some. She turned him every which way but loose. Upside down, inside out, he lost all sense of direction and time and spatial relationships. He lost all sense of everything except her moist, heated mouth.

Languidly Eden massaged every inch of the front of his body. From his head to his navel to his knees to his toes.

Everywhere, that is, except for his throbbing cock.

Where had she learned such incredible maneuvers? He'd been around the block a few times, but he'd never experienced anything like this. The woman was a tantalizing temptress with more talents up her sleeve than a full-service geisha.

Maybe with a woman like this marriage wouldn't be dull and boring.

Whoa!

What in the hell was he thinking? Marriage? Ridiculous. This affair was supposed to make him *stop* thinking about getting married. Randy and Jill's breakup served as a realistic reminder that sex was sex and love was, well…messy and unpredictable and painful. He wanted no part of it, but man, did he want more of this. More of her. He wanted inside her so badly he could taste his own raw, salty lust.

Then Eden reached out and tickled his penis with her gloved hand and his mind exploded into acute carnal awareness.

Her rhythm was firm, smooth and steady. It was as if she knew exactly how he liked to be stroked.

In a matter of seconds, he was ready to come, but she stopped just as he hovered on the edge of climax.

He groaned and feared the pressure of his unfulfilled desire would blow the top of his head off. And even though he throbbed in a deliciously painful way, he was glad he'd agreed to act out this fantasy. It was far superior to anything he'd ever conjured in his wildest imaginings.

She waited a few minutes. Until his breathing slowed, his pulse went down to a rate resembling normal and his erection abated.

And then she returned for a second round.

In the ensuing interim, she'd discarded the gloves and lubed her hands with something warm and oily and scented with cinnamon. He moaned when she wrapped those skillful fingers around his shaft and kneaded him like bread dough.

She rolled him in her palms, then pressed his penis against his pelvis and stroked the underside. Next, she made two rings with a thumb and index finger of each slippery hot hand, placed them next to each other in the middle of his shaft and gently pulled outward in both directions at once.

The sensation of being stretched into two pieces was incredible. He made a strangled sound of pleasure.

"You like?"

He couldn't speak, so he simply nodded.

"You've got a gorgeous cock. It looks very tasty."

When she brought her lips to the head of him, Alec literally arched off the bed, the damned bindings anchored him to the bedposts when all he wanted to do was rip off the ropes and get at her.

Playfully she licked him and then discovered the ridge that ran down the underside of his penis, and she skipped her tongue along it and across it. Pointing her tongue, she flicked with pinpoint focus over the ridge, strumming him like a banjo.

She seemed to love what she was doing. Her excited little moans shoved him into a whole new state of advanced arousal. It was as if she couldn't get enough of tasting his manhood. She used her mouth like a very imaginative and agile vagina, covering her teeth with her lips so she wouldn't accidentally nick him, and slowly she slid his penis into the recesses of her mouth.

Was there a more wonderful, seductive woman in the whole of creation? He didn't see how there could be.

She moved her head up and down, smoothly and continuously. She wiggled her tongue back and forth across his quivering shaft and probed the slit on top.

Delicious!

When she tightened her hands around the base

while she kept gently sucking, he knew he was done for and dammit, he still hadn't given her an orgasm. He didn't want it like this. He did not!

But too late, he felt the heat and pressure rushing up, up, up to greet her.

A yellow-hot heat blasted through the base of his brain, searing him so severely he could not form a single rational thought.

"I'm on the brink, Eden," he gasped. "I'm on the brink."

And just like that she stopped.

For a moment, he hung between release and defeat. Then he crash-landed—boom, without spilling his essence. He was happy and perturbed all at the same time. He groaned loud enough to rattle the windows in the hotel lobby.

"Now," she said, "you catch your breath, because then it's my turn."

"Yes," he hissed through clenched teeth, fighting against the pain of his interrupted climax. "It's your turn. Bring yourself up here and I'll lick you for all you're worth." He touched his tongue to his lips, eager for the taste of her feminine richness.

"No," she said. "I'm going to get myself ready for you with a blow-by-blow commentary."

"Blow by blow?" he said weakly.

She was situated between his legs and he could feel her bare buttocks brushing either side of his thigh.

"Uh-huh, pun intended."

"I'm listening." He strained his ears and vividly imagined what she began to describe.

"I'm wetting my fingers with warm massage oil."

"Uh-huh."

"The oil is dripping off my fingers onto my belly."

He clenched his teeth, stifling yet another groan.

"Oh," she whispered. "That feels good."

"What does?"

"I'm running two fingers across my clit."

He almost choked as his mind supplied him with a very colorful picture.

"Oh, yeah."

Alec felt her buttocks contract as she moved. "What now?"

"I'm all hot and swollen and achy."

"Me too, babe, me too."

"I'm gliding my fingers over my wet, throbbing lips. I'm pretending it's your penis, slipping in and out of me, in and out."

Not being able to watch her pleasure herself was driving him right over the cliff of primal madness. He bucked and thrashed, tossing his head in an attempt to dislodge the blindfold, but no such luck.

"Ooh," she moaned, and rocked against his thighs. "Oh yeah."

"That's it. Love yourself. You are so beautiful and sexy and daring."

"Uh-uh-uh-uh," she gasped.

He'd never heard a more erotic sound in his life. "What's happening now?"

"I'm pinching my nipple with my other hand. It feels so good."

"Have mercy on me, babe," he begged, and

thrashed harder against the bindings. If only he could get one hand free, he could regain control of the situation. "I can't stand this one second more. I want to be inside you so bad it hurts. Please, Eden, please. I want to make you come."

"You want me to ride you?"

"Yes! Untie me. I want to touch you."

"No. You are my boy toy and you must do as I say."

He let loose with a curse then. Not cursing her, but cursing himself for agreeing to this. While he loved what was happening to him, his frustration at not being able to touch her naked body knew no limits.

"Okay, fine, forget the ropes, just ride me."

"Gotta get a condom." She left the bed but quickly returned to expertly sheathe him with a rubber.

And then she made it worse, teasing him yet again. Her knees pinned his hips, his erection jutted up, pleading, but rather than sinking down on him, she hovered. He could feel her body heat but not her sweet wetness.

He wanted to clutch her around the waist and force her down, but he couldn't. Alec was compelled to keep waiting.

Patience, patience, don't be selfish.

Just when he had steeled himself for more relentless teasing, Eden slid slickly over this penis.

He gasped and shuddered. Nothing had ever, ever, felt this good.

Nothing.

She was so tight and hot and wonderful.

Their coupling was wild, frantic, crazed. She rode him hard and fast and desperate.

Together they flew, soaring upward. He was blind and could not see. He was tied and could not move. He was captured.

And he loved what she was doing to him.

Her flesh was smooth and soft and tender and he realized with a start she had no hair down there. The woman had waxed far more than her bikini line!

And he didn't think he could take any more surprises.

Eden was wild and willing. She encompassed him with her plush womanly body. He could picture her with her head tossed back, her pelvis arched, her hair trailing down her spine in a spiral of chestnut curls.

Ride, baby, ride.

She squeezed him with her love muscles. Wave after rhythmic wave. Clenching and releasing, clenching and releasing.

Streams of pleasure shot through him like whitewater rapids, sending him plunging over into the abyss at the same time she screamed his name.

Never had there been an orgasm like the one that ricocheted through his body. His two previously thwarted climaxes coalesced into one colossal release. He felt it everywhere. In his groin, in his brain, in his chest, in his toes. It sang through his blood and bounced off his bones.

She collapsed against his chest, their bodies drenched in sweat. They lay gasping for the longest time, just trying to catch their breath. Finally, when their heart rates had slowed, Eden rolled off him.

"That was…" she panted, "totally awesome."

"The best ever."

"No kidding?"

"Babe, you have no idea."

She scrambled over him and he heard her feet hit the floor. A few minutes later she had the ropes untied. He pulled off the blindfold, eager to see her in the fresh flush of lovemaking.

He was disappointed to discover she had gotten dressed. He reached out, grabbed her and pulled her to his chest. Next time, it was his turn to hitch her to the bedposts and give as good as he'd gotten.

"See." She raised the hourglass in triumph. "The sand ran out a long time ago. You lasted well over an hour. From now on, bring the hourglass with you whenever we meet."

"Whatever you say."

She lay down beside him, one ear positioned over his heart. He trailed a hand through her hair, disadvantaged with her dressed and him still buck naked.

"You're a cruel wench, Eden Montgomery," he murmured, stroking her cheek. "Tying me down, taking away my control, torturing me."

"You loved it."

He was so drunk on the moment, so captivated by Eden's experimentation and creativity, he almost said, *I love you,* but he bit down on his tongue in the nick of time.

What the hell was that?

A panicky sensation dropped through him. Of course, he didn't love her. He liked her. An incredible amount. She stimulated him in a way no woman ever had and he loved what she was doing to him. But he simply wasn't the kind of guy who fell in love. He preferred to keep things light and commitment free. Love complicated everything. Just ask Randy.

RANDY STERLING SAT on a bar stool at Bombshells, staring morosely into the overpriced beer he'd been nursing for the past hour. He hadn't been inside the raunchy strip club since he'd met Jill over a year ago.

Sighing, he shook his head. He still didn't know what had gone wrong. Everything had been perfect between them until that damned wedding shower.

Not too perfect, if you didn't even know she was unhappy.

He took a swig of his beer. Hell, Alec was right. Women. Who could figure 'em? The more you tried to please them the less you succeeded.

For Jill, he'd even given up sex. And it had been his idea. He'd wanted to prove to her that he had changed. That he was no longer that immature playboy who saw love and commitment as a noose around a man's neck. Once he met her, he had *wanted* love and marriage and happily-ever-after and just when it seemed he had it all—*ka-blewy.*

A red-haired woman in a tight-fitting leather skirt sauntered over to sit beside him. He sighed. She was the fifth one he'd had to chase away since he'd arrived.

What in the hell was he doing here? he wondered with a jolt. He'd thought a drink and watching nearly naked ladies twirl on the catwalk would send his blues packing. It hadn't.

"Hi there, big fella." The redhead spoke in a soft purr. She had to lean in close to his shoulder in order to be heard above the throbbing dance music.

Randy didn't even look up from peeling the label off his longneck.

"You look like you could use some cheering up."

He turned his head toward her, but still did not glance at her face. "Look, I'm sure you're a very nice lady, but I'm just not interested."

She reached over, took his hand and laid it on her bare knee. He looked down and almost yanked his hand away but something about that knee looked very familiar.

"Sometimes," she said in a voice he recognized. "What we need to solve our problems is nothing more than hot sex with a total stranger."

He jerked his head up and met those soft brown eyes he knew so well.

But the sexy tilt of her head, the wide scarlet slash of lipstick adorning her lips, the saucy attitude of a thoroughly bad girl was startlingly new and different. Instantly his cock hardened and his heart careened in his chest.

"Jill?" he whispered, scarcely about to believe this sexy vamp was his quiet, reserved fiancée.

"No," she said. "My name is Candy. And if you want to try something sweet, then come with me."

Stunned, he simply stared at her openmouthed. What on earth had possessed his demure woman to behave so provocatively?

Not that he was complaining.

She stood up, took his hand and urged him off his bar stool.

"Jill…Candy…what are you up to? Are you sure you…"

"Shh." She pressed a manicured finger to her lips. "Come with me."

Dumbfounded, Randy allowed her to lead him through the dimly lit club. He watched her fanny sway, and his blood pressure shot through the top of his head as the million X-rated thoughts he'd managed to keep under control while they were dating kaleidoscoped into a vivid montage in his mind's eye.

Tugging on his hand, she pushed open the door to the ladies' rest room.

"What's this?" he asked, surprised to find his voice coming out reedy and tight and excited. "What's going on?"

"No talking."

Randy stared at her in disbelief. Who *was* this woman? He'd known Jill for over a year and it turns out he didn't know her at all.

Luckily the bathroom was empty. She led him into a wide stall and locked the door behind them. Prudence urged him to set her aside and bolt from the room, but he didn't stand a chance in hell of making his legs move when she was rubbing her breasts against his chest and unzipping his zipper.

Every nerve, every muscle, every cell in his body strained toward her at the same time she pushed him against the wall of the stall with a desperate, unexpected strength.

She plastered her long, lean body against his, wound her arms around his neck and wrapped one leg around his waist.

"I'm not wearing any panties," she hissed, and at the very same time she lightly bit his bottom lip.

Randy growled low in his throat and surrendered to the challenge. He inhaled her scent, at once familiar and different. New cologne, new clothes, but beneath it all, the woman he loved. A woman with unexpected tricks tucked inside her silky sleeves.

Her breasts flattened into his chest, burning him through the thin lace blouse she wore and proving to him she was braless.

He plunged his tongue deep inside the warmth of her open mouth. She tasted of heated butterscotch but sweeter, slicker, hotter. He couldn't get enough of her flavor, all Jill and yet not. He cupped the back of her head in his palms, keeping her pinned into place while he pillaged her mouth.

A year's worth of celibacy exploded into a crazed, blind intensity he could not control. Jill attacked him. Shoving his jeans down over his hips, running her hands over him, nibbling his neck.

Her wild movements drove him insane. This wasn't how it was supposed to go. Wasn't how he'd planned for their first time.

Plans were made to be broken.

"Take me now, stud."

Yes. Yes.

He didn't think. He just lifted her up by the waist, while balancing himself precariously against the stall door, and lowered her down onto his throbbing erection.

She was wet and slick and ready, but when he met with resistance, he stopped, suddenly confused. What were they doing?

"Don't stop." She clawed his back. "Give it to me. Now! I want your hot cock."

Her rabid lust took possession of him, swept him away. If this was what she wanted, he would give it to her. He pulled her down tight on his erection.

She cried out. "Oh, oh."

"I'm hurting you."

She thrashed her head. "Keep going. I want this. I want you."

He stared into her face and his heart tore as realization dawn. "Jill," he said. Tears welled up in his eyes and jumbled emotions ripped through his chest. "You're a virgin."

11

"TELL ME YOUR SECRETS," Alec whispered to her in the dark.

They lay cuddled together on the bed following their session of body-numbing, mind-blowing sex, and Eden had been trying to work up the energy to pry herself from his warmth and go home.

"Huh?" she asked drowsily.

"Your secrets. What are they?"

For one long moment she feared he was talking about her scar. Her breath ran from her body in short little gasps and her heart rate sped up. She opened her mouth to tell him about the fire and the night that had changed her life forever, but no words came out.

And then she realized that, in spite of what they'd shared, in spite of the fact she liked him far more than she suspected she should, she still was not ready to fully expose her vulnerability to him. She still did not trust him completely.

Would she ever?

The old paranoia crept in. Her fear of getting hurt was far greater than her desire for intimacy.

She couldn't show him. Not yet.

But you've only got a week left.

Thank heavens for that. Thank heavens, she'd had the foresight to slap a time limit on their affair. Because she knew if she kept seeing him, she would fall in love with him. She was already halfway there and she knew she needed much more than Alec could ever offer.

"Tell me—" he raked his fingers through her curls and lightly kissed her forehead "—where did you learn such exotic tricks?"

Oh, *those* secrets.

Relieved, she inhaled deeply. "I read a lot."

"Babe, the things you just did to me with your tongue require more than just reading. You've had practice."

Guilty as charged, but she wasn't about to tell him she'd taken Jayne's advice and practiced on a banana.

"You know just how to keep a man intrigued," Alec said. "Never revealing too much, hiding behind that sly smile."

If only he knew! He was the reason she'd emerged from her chrysalis. Because of him and the necessity of retrieving her creativity. She couldn't separate the two events—the resurgence of her imagination and her attraction to Alec Ramsey would always be fused in her mind.

"In fact," he murmured, "I've been doing some serious thinking."

"Uh-oh, sounds dangerous. Spontaneous guy wielding a deep thought," she teased, but her chest tightened again.

"Yeah. I'm taking a big chance here. Going out on a limb."

"Now that sounds like you."

"Let's extend things," he blurted.

"What do you mean?"

"These past few weeks have been very special."

"Yes."

"I want to keep seeing you." His breath fanned her cheek.

Eden's heart stilled, her mind a crazy tilt of what-ifs.

What if she said yes?

Bad idea. Very bad. What if you lose your heart?

What if she didn't?

"I'm sorry, Alec. I thought I was quite clear about my stipulations when we started this."

"You were. It's just that…"

"There's nothing to be gained by seeing each other for a longer period of time."

"We could have more fun. What's wrong with that?" He rubbed a knuckle across her lips.

"Everything must come to an end," she said, sounding much tougher than she felt. "It's been great fun, but next Saturday is our last day together."

. "So why wait until next Saturday?" he asked. "Why not end it now?"

He had her there. Why *not* end it now? She'd already learned a lot, grown bold, explored her sexuality. She'd gotten her creativity back. He had already taught her a great deal about herself. What would one more week accomplish?

Involuntarily, her hand went to her lower abdomen and she knew why she could not end things tonight. She still hadn't accomplished the one thing that caused her the most distress. She still hadn't been able to let him see her completely naked.

"Wow, EDEN. You've outdone yourself." Ashley stared at the newest Spice-Up-Your-Love-Life Cruises gift basket design, an expression of awe on her face. "I gotta hand it to you, linking up with Alec has done heinously brilliant things for your creativity."

"You really think it's that good?" Eden felt her cheeks flush with pleasure over her assistant's open admiration. The end-of-the-month deadline was upon her, but she was satisfied with her work.

"Definitely hot." Ashley fingered the shredded leather miniskirt Eden had used as a liner for the battered Harley hubcap that provided the crucible. "The two leather masks connected face-to-face by a strip of red velvet ribbon, whew." Ashley fanned herself with a hand.

"Simulated kissing."

"I get that. The Chambord is a nice touch. Trend setting. And the flashy, trashy color scheme has an urban decay chic thing going on."

"I tried hard to merge sexy with hip and cutting edge."

"You succeeded big time. And I love the name. Ménage à Masquerade."

"Thanks."

Eden had put the finishing touches on the design after her night with Alec. Something had been missing from the basket, but she hadn't been able to put her finger on exactly what it was until he'd started talking about secrets and hidden identities and clandestine agendas. That's when she had added the masks and fingerless gloves and then wrapped the entire arrangement with a black mesh veil.

The minute she finished the basket, she knew Tori Drake was going to love it. Now, if only the powers-that-be at Spice-Up-Your-Love-Life Cruises bought into her concept of edgy.

And speaking of edgy, she was still feeling nervous from last night's love fest with Alec, not to mention deliciously sore.

Just then the front door was flung open and Jill Fincher rushed into the boutique. Her eyes danced with excitement and she was dressed in a sexy champagne-colored stretch-silk shirt and matching silk pants.

Who knew the woman possessed such a red-hot figure?

"Eden!" she cried. "The wedding's back on and it's all thanks to you!"

"Me?"

"I took your advice and it worked to a tee. I dressed up like a stripper and seduced Randy in the ladies' room at Bombshells. The sex was out of this world."

"When you go out on a limb you really go out on a limb." Eden grinned at her.

Jill looked so happy, pride welled in Eden's chest. To think she had had a hand in Jill's sexual awakening.

"You took sex advice from Eden?" Ashley asked.

"Sure. Why not?" Jill glanced from Ashley to Eden, and back again.

Ashley smirked, shook her head and went back to folding thongs. "All I gotta say is, Eden Montgomery, you've changed."

"Oh!" Jill said, distracted by the Spice-Up-Your-Love-Life basket. "Is this your latest creation?"

"Uh-huh."

"It's incredible. Oh my goodness, is that what I think it is?"

Eden nodded. "The rabbit, as seen on *Sex and the City*."

"You are so creative."

Not without Alec, I'm not.

Now that was stupid. Of course she didn't need Alec to stay in the creative groove. He was the dynamite who'd removed her block, but that was all.

Right?

"Anyway, I dropped by to tell you, you're invited to the wedding. It's next Saturday at three in New Haven. Here's the address." Jill handed her an engraved invitation.

Next Saturday? But that was supposed to be her last day with Alec. Which meant, of course, he would be at the wedding and not meeting her for their final hurrah at the Grand Duchess.

"Jill, that's so sweet of you, but I'm afraid I'm not going to be able to make it."

The mere thought of seeing Alec at a wedding, surrounded by his adoring family and friends, caused her heart to perform a wild, skittering dance. Too schmaltzy for comfort. And besides, she didn't trust herself. She was on the verge of falling in love with him and something like watching a happy couple exchange vows could shove her over the edge.

The last thing she needed was to go soft in the head over a man married to bachelorhood.

Jill looked disappointed. "That's too bad. I was so looking forward to having you there. If you change your mind, the offer stands."

"Thank you."

"No, thank *you*." Jill leaned over to give her a hug.

Eden hugged her back then walked her new friend to the door. As she watched her leave, she realized Tuesday night with Alec would be her last.

HE NEEDED a grand seduction scheme. A no-fail plan to guarantee Eden would agree to extend their affair. He couldn't understand why she was so adamant about sticking to this one-month time frame. It was nonsense. They were both having a good time and they hadn't begun to scratch the surface of their sexual adventures together.

There were so many things they hadn't yet tried.

Alec wanted to sleep with her on a blanket stretched out on a sandy beach. He wanted to make her tingle with ecstasy as they made love on the desk in his office. He was dying to do it in the woods, in a swimming pool, in an elevator. He fantasized about taking her warm, willing body on a mountain, in the rain, on a sailboat.

But most of all, he wanted to see her completely naked. To admire that luscious body she coyly and mysteriously cloaked in shadows and costumes. He wanted to see her in full sunlight. With mirrors. He wanted to gaze at her body and watch her respond to his touch.

She'd shown him she was up for almost anything and that knowledge excited him even more. He was determined to make his fantasies come true.

His mission—to show her such a wonderful time she would be unable to resist continuing their relationship. But he needed a foolproof plan and he was coming up empty.

Then when Randy burst into his office, grinning ear to ear and spouting wild stories about Jill and the ladies' room at Bombshells and the wedding being back on, Alec recognized the way to achieve his goal—keep Eden off balance the same way she'd knocked him lopsided with her devilish tricks.

Leave her begging for more.

He told Holden to call Wickedly Wonderful and tell Eden he couldn't keep their Tuesday night appointment and then he sat back in his chair to wait.

Not five minutes passed before his telephone jangled.

"Alec?" Eden sounded breathless, anxious and

disappointed. A little huff of air rolled down the phone lines and tickled his ear. Her cute little noise had him ready to cave, but he held firm.

It was like reeling in a swordfish. Jerk too hard, move too soon and you've lost her.

"Speaking."

"You're canceling on me for tomorrow night?"

"Sorry, sweetheart, but something's come up." He hated fibbing to her, but he assured himself it was for a greater good.

"Oh."

"Is something wrong?" he asked.

"I suppose you'll be going to Randy and Jill's wedding on Saturday. I won't see you then either."

"I'm Randy's best man."

"Of course. You do realize that our four weeks are up on Saturday."

His stomach lurched at the despair in her voice. Alec reminded himself this was the only way he'd convince her to come to New Haven with him for the weekend.

"I know. And it's such a shame we won't get to see each other one last time." He grinned at his manipulations and struggled to keep the amusement from his tone. She was going for it. He could practically feel her wavering.

She hitched in her breath. Was she as hot and horny as he? Starving for one last fling. He hoped it was true.

"Unless…" he enticed.

"We can't extend," she said brusquely.

"Just a thought." Alec shrugged and his hopes plummeted.

A long silence ensued and then he dropped the proposal. Subtle, sort of casual, nothing too obvious that might tip her off about how desperate he was to see her again.

"You know, you could come to the wedding. Randy told me you're invited."

She inhaled sharply and he could almost see her worrying her bottom lip with her teeth.

How he wished she were here. What he wouldn't give to kiss those sweet raspberry-colored lips of hers. To breathe in her scent. To snuggle her long, smooth neck.

Just thinking about the pale, snowy scoop of skin between her gold-studded earlobes and her slender collarbone launched him into orbit.

"We could rent a room at a quaint little B and B on the beach. Spend the weekend. Make up for missing tomorrow night. Our last tango, so to speak."

Still, she said nothing.

"Just a thought. If you wouldn't really feel comfortable at a wedding, I understand. Weddings make me nervous, too."

Would his ploy work? Would she take the bait?

"Alec...I..."

"I guess this is goodbye," he said softly and his gut squeezed.

It's just because she's so hot and you're going to miss the great sex, he told himself, but that still didn't explain the heavy pressure crowding his chest. *She's*

*a special woman for certain, but you've got nothing
to offer her beyond a good time. She deserves more
than you can give. Let her go.*

He cleared his throat, no longer playing the game.
If she didn't want to see him, it was better to cut
things off now. "I gotta go."

"Wait!"

He froze with his hand halfway to the phone cradle.
Slowly he brought the receiver back to his ear. "I'm
still here."

"Okay," she said. "All right. I'll spend the weekend in New Haven with you."

THE FIRST SATURDAY in November turned out perfect
for an afternoon wedding. The air was crisp but not
too cold. The last fall colors on the southern coast of
Connecticut remained a stunning palette of gold,
bronze, scarlet, mahogany and peach.

The church spire was nestled between brilliant ma-
ples, and a singular group of white birches were set
off by a white picket fence. The smell of wood smoke
filled the air, and in the distance came the sounds of
a high school football team running drills before the
big game. The sky was a cerulean blue with clouds
so white and fluffy they appeared surreal.

Alec had picked her up that morning in his Ferrari.
Eden was so nervous she'd resorted to rubbing the
worry stone. A couple of times on the drive up he
mentioned continuing their affair, but each time she'd
gently turned him down. The longer she spent with

him the likelier it was that he would break her heart. Her ticker already felt a little tender.

They checked into the B and B and then went on over to the church. Jill, Sarah and the rest of Alec's family greeted her with enthusiastic hugs, and Eden was surprised and delighted to find Jayne Lockerbee and her husband Roger among the guests.

Eden sat next to Jayne and Roger toward the back of the church. When Alec appeared at the altar alongside Randy, all her doubts disappeared and she was glad she had come, even though she was scared and excited about what lay ahead of them at the B and B.

When Jill appeared looking like the cover of *Bride* magazine, Eden almost burst into tears.

Jayne squeezed Eden's hand and leaned over to whisper, "One day soon, it'll be your turn."

Eden smiled and a sadness tugged her heart. What a mess! The only person she could imagine marrying was the man who could never settle down. The same man who'd given her the courage to really explore her sexuality. The man she would never have as her own.

Fumbling in the pocket of the blue silk dress she'd purchased for the occasion, Eden fingered the smooth, soothing surface of the worry stone and instantly felt herself grow calmer. Everything was going to be all right, no matter what happened between her and Alec. She was tough. She was strong. She could survive any worst-case scenario her mind dreamed up.

She realized then exactly how much she'd changed over the past month. Thanks to Alec. While she would never be completely spontaneous and light-hearted, a bit of his devil-may-care attitude had rubbed off on her. She was a better person for having known him and she would be forever grateful.

Swallowing her tears, she tried to pay attention to the ceremony, but found her gaze fixed on the back of Alec's neck.

He'd gotten a haircut, she noticed, and she missed the curl of dark hair at his collar.

His broad shoulders were accentuated by the excellent fit of his tuxedo, and a swoony tightness filled her lungs.

When Randy turned to greet his bride, Alec turned, too. He looked out into the crowd and caught her eye. A slight smile tipped the corners of his lips and set Eden's heart into a headlong, whimpering rhythm.

Unnerved by the restless sensations roaming her body, Eden dropped her gaze. By the time she looked up again, the wedding party was facing the minister.

She forced herself to focus on Randy and Jill. They looked so happy. Eden was glad she'd been able to help Jill overcome her feelings of inadequacy. The door of communication had been thrown wide open and she knew in her heart those two would make it.

Just as she knew she and Alec could never be more than two ships passing in the night. It was enough for her. Alec had made sure she knew from the very beginning that he was the kind of guy who kept his options open. Marriage never figured into the equation for him. Which was just fine with her.

She wasn't looking to get married. All she'd

wanted was to regain her creativity and explore her femininity and vanquish her fears about her scars. She'd done the first two and, after tonight, she would have accomplished everything she'd set out to accomplish when she'd entered into this temporary relationship.

She was going to make full use of her newfound sense of adventure. She was going to party, have fun and forget all about the future. Nothing mattered but the moment. As Alec had taught her, nothing mattered except enjoying yourself.

She refused to have any regrets.

ALEC STOOD beside Randy, surprised to discover he could not concentrate on the ceremony. He thought, when this moment came, he would be filled with sadness over losing his buddy and business partner to marriage. Instead, he couldn't seem to keep his mind off Eden.

One glance over his shoulder and he'd spotted her immediately. When their eyes met he felt a strange sort of stabbing sensation deep within him. It was because of that silky blue dress she had on, he assured himself. It was impossible not to stare and wonder if she wore any lingerie beneath the thin, shimmery material.

The dress molded to her form, fit tightly across her bustline, nipped in at her slender waist and flared out over those dynamite hips.

Hold on, Ramsey. You'll be undressing her soon

enough. He forced himself to rip his stare away from her and return his attention to the minister.

Jill was gazing at Randy as if he'd painted the stars in the sky just for her. As for Randy, his buddy was floating on cloud nine.

Didn't it bother them, he wondered, that by getting married they were narrowing their choices? Randy had locked himself into a gigantic commitment.

Alec shook his head at the consequences of marriage. No more spontaneous trips to scale mountains with his buddies. No more opportunities to sleep with ravishing beauties who piqued his interest. No more partying until the wee hours of the morning.

No more fun. No more freedom.

His best friend had forsaken it all.

And yet when Alec watched Randy and his new bride together, he couldn't help thinking maybe the path Randy had chosen wasn't so bad after all.

Damn! What had him thinking this way? His hot, fun, mischievous affair with Eden was supposed to have cured the wistfulness he'd felt over Randy's marriage. Instead, his once vague sense of dissatisfaction mushroomed.

Being here with Eden among his family and friends stirred up feelings he never knew he possessed. She had him thinking that maybe it was possible to settle down and still have fun. That surrendering his freedom for a lifetime of love wasn't the worst thing that could happen to a guy.

No other woman had ever caused Alec to take stock of his life like this. No other woman had ever gotten under his skin and made him itch to be with her. No other woman had tied him so completely in knots.

Bringing Eden to New Haven had been a horrible mistake.

Helplessly he cast another quick glance over his shoulder as the minister told Randy he could kiss his bride.

He caught Eden studying him.

Her face flushed and a sense of dread spread through him like a stone dropped into a pool. She was ensnared by their chemical attraction just as surely as he.

His mouth automatically filled with moisture. He was like one of Pavlov's dogs. Stimulus and response. Looking at her made him yearn for something he could not express. Something that scared the living hell out of him.

Eden winked and gave him a wicked little smile that promised hours and hours of sexual delight just as soon as she got him back to the B and B.

Run! Flee! Take off! His old avoidance patterns kicked him hard in the gut.

Uh-oh. He was in serious trouble here. Alec felt as if he had dived headfirst from an airplane at six thousand feet without a parachute. He was going to hit the ground.

Splat!

And it was going to hurt more than he could ever imagine.

12

"CONGRATULATIONS," Uncle Mac said, slapping Alec on the back at the reception and then passing him a flute of champagne.

"Congratulations? I'm not the one who just got married."

"I'm referring to your date." His uncle nodded toward the dance floor, where Eden was getting pretty jiggy with it, shaking her booty in time to "Respect" along with his sisters and a gaggle of other women. The guys had deserted the dance floor with that tune. "Look at her go."

She swung her hips like a pendulum and waved her arms over her head. The hem of her blue silk dress inched up her thighs revealing a yard of gorgeous legs. Men on the sidelines drooled appreciatively and he had the sudden urge to smack each and every gawker right in the mouth. He knew what they were thinking as they watched her dance. He had a sexual bonfire of his own blazing in his shorts.

Eden dipped and swayed and giggled.

Exactly how many of those potent tequila sunrises had she sucked down?

Alec pressed the champagne flute to his forehead,

praying the cool drink would send his temperature down a notch or two. It was all he could do not to march across that dance floor, scoop her into his arms and whisk her away.

He thought of what he had in store for her back at the B and B. Candles, soft music and satin sheets. He wanted it quiet and sweet and tender. Tonight was not about hard, hot sex. Tonight he wanted to gently romance her. To show her how much these past few weeks had meant to him. Tonight was all about her.

"Yep," Mac said. "She's a wild one. Good work on picking someone who's not interested in throwing a lasso over you, the way Jill snared Randy. Eden is all about the fun."

"Who says she's not interested in a serious relationship?"

Mac blinked. "Why, she did. When we were doing the chicken dance, she told me you were the perfect boy toy. That bothers you? I'd have figured you'd be overjoyed to have a woman who wasn't the least bit interested in settling down."

"I am."

"Funny, you look kind of mad."

Boy toy. Alec gritted his teeth. He wasn't a toy and he certainly wasn't a boy. Had she actually said that? Was that all he was to her?

Wasn't that all you wanted to be?

Yes. No.

Holy crap. He was in trouble here. If he had a lick of sense he'd haul her cute little fanny back to Manhattan so fast it would make her dizzy.

Unfortunately, where Eden was concerned it seemed he possessed no brains at all. When they'd arrived at the reception, Eden had whispered in his ears, "Buy me a drink, big guy. I'm ready to party."

He'd complied, happy for her to have a good time, but somewhere along the way, between the oglers and Eden's uninhibited sway, he'd changed his mind.

When had he gotten so stuffy? And so possessive? If it had been any other woman he'd dated he would be out on the dance floor living it up with her rather than brooding on the sidelines.

What *was* wrong with him?

The next thing he knew, the deejay had put Gloria Estefan on the sound system and started a conga line right behind Eden.

They undulated through the crowd, tugging people into the conga line as they went, Eden leading the way, the good-looking deejay's hands clasped around her narrow waist.

Alec didn't want anyone's hands on her except his own. Glowering, he shoved his glass of champagne at Mac and stalked toward the conga line.

Eden's eyes met his. She sent him a sly, secretive smile and darted out her tongue to touch her upper lip and slowly wag it back and forth. The pressure in his pants increased exponentially with each sassy swish of her tongue. When had the woman become such an outrageous flirt?

He liked it and yet he did not.

Gloria Estefan invited everyone to do the conga.

Eden reached out to him but, rather than take her

hand and get in front of her, Alec clamped a hand on her waist above the startled deejay's hand and, like an ill-mannered motorist forcing his SUV into five-o'clock traffic, he wedged his body between Eden and the other man.

With a quick turn of her head, Eden flashed him another smile. "Jealous?" she whispered.

"Why would I be jealous?" he growled. "Just because you're shaking your booty so hard the men are getting whiplash from watching you."

"And what's wrong with that?" She laughed and saucily swished her fanny, snaking the conga line along with her as she danced around the tables and chairs.

Did she have any idea what she was doing to him?

Probably. In fact, driving him crazy was no doubt all part of her evil master plan. If she kept up that swishing he'd have to steal a tablecloth to hide his erection.

Thankfully, the conga music ended and the deejay hustled back to the dais to round up recruits for a rousing rendition of "YMCA."

But before Alec had time to pull Eden aside and ask if she would like to leave the reception early, his four sisters and Jill descended upon them.

"Can we borrow Eden for a minute?" His youngest sister Diana asked.

Alec opened his mouth to protest, but could think of no excuse strong enough to deter five women giddy with champagne and happy endings. He knew when he was outnumbered.

"Sure. No problem." He forced a smile. "I'll just wait right here."

"We were hoping you could keep Mac company and steer him clear of Randy," Jill said.

"He's had too much too drink," Sarah explained. "And he's over there carping about the perils of marriage. Poor guy." She shook her head. "He just turned fifty and he still hasn't grown up."

Alec felt a strange stab of emotion as he realized his beloved uncle had become something of a caricature of the lonely, has-been playboy. He swallowed hard. "Okay, sure." Struggling to appear nonchalant, he meandered away from the ladies when all he wanted to do was throw Eden over his shoulder caveman-style and make off with her.

"WHAT'S UP?" Eden asked as her friends dragged her off to the powder room with them.

"Alec is." Sarah giggled. "In case you hadn't noticed. I've never seen him so smitten."

Eden felt her face flush flamingo-pink. "He's not smitten, he's just horny."

"Trust me on this. We've seen the women come and the women go and Alec has never acted jealous before. He is definitely smitten with you." Kylie grinned.

Eden's heart crowded her chest. Could it be true? Did she dare hope that she meant more to Alec than a casual fling? He *did* keep pressing her to extend their affair, but how could she be sure? And did she want to be with a man who had trouble with commitment, even if he was smitten as his sisters claimed.

Besides, he hadn't yet seen her scars. That might change everything.

The worry and anxiety she'd shed and kept at bay with tequila sunrises and lots of dancing, came spilling back. She realized her new friends were trying to help, but she'd made her peace with Alec's role in her life. He was her love mentor and nothing more. Their assertions that he was infatuated with her muddled her mind and increased her chances of ending up with a broken heart.

Maybe she should just catch the train home and forget about spending the rest of the weekend with him. It was the smart thing to do.

Eden shook her head. "You guys are reading too much into this. Alec and I are nothing more than..." She almost said *fuck buddies* but bit down on her tongue.

No. That phrase didn't adequately reflect their relationship. They weren't really buddies. They were lovers and temporary ones at that. Fuck buddies were friends who helped each other out in a sexual pinch. Fuck buddies eased frustration.

If anything, Alec added to her sexual aggravations. No matter how much time they spent together, she couldn't seem to get enough. Her need for him was as strong as an addiction and twice as scary. Why else had she agreed to a weekend in Connecticut?

"You could be the one who brings him to his knees," Diana said.

"He escorted you to a wedding," Alison pointed out. "That means something."

Little did Alison know that her brother's invitation meant only one thing. Sex. Without a doubt, Eden knew if it hadn't been their last Saturday together, Alec would not have brought her to the wedding.

She'd already picked up on his irritation and she was confused about what his broodiness meant. She thought he had wanted her to act wild and carefree and when she had done just what he wished, he'd gotten all pouty and possessive.

Well, too bad! Once she'd tasted the freedom of ditching her insecurities she wasn't going back to being afraid. She was taking that final step tonight and the consequences be damned.

ALEC COULDN'T WAIT to get Eden back to the B and B. The wedding reception seemed to drag on forever. When Jill tossed the bouquet and it landed at Eden's feet, Sarah plucked the delicate flower arrangement from the floor and thrust it into Eden's hand.

He was oddly disconcerted when Eden shoved the bouquet at Kylie and said, "You take it. I'm not about to be the next one married." He should be *glad* that marriage was the last thing on her mind, not vaguely disappointed.

Finally, finally, Jill and Randy left for their hotel and people began filtering out of the reception room. When Eden raised up on her toes to press her lips to his ear and whispered, "Let's get the hell out of here," Alec just about came unhinged.

He sucked in a quick breath and his pulse jackhammered as her sweet womanly scent filled his nostrils. The rest of the weekend stretched out before them like a long, languid ribbon of highway just waiting to be traversed. And he couldn't think of anyone else on earth he'd rather traverse it with.

Taking her hand, he guided her around the other guests, slipping away into the crowd and heading toward his Ferrari glistening darkly in the dim glow of the parking lot vapor lamps. The ocean stretched out past the pier, blue and deep and the low, earthy sound of a passing ship's foghorn vibrated the night air.

His imagination raced ahead of him. Sprinting to the B and B, leading Eden into their bedroom, slowly undressing her. Tonight, he'd already decided, was going to be special. No gadgets, no games, no toys. Just he and Eden together, making love slow, soft and easy.

He couldn't wait to see her naked body, couldn't wait to run his fingertips over her bare skin, couldn't wait to taste the salty flavor of her womanly essence.

Beside him sat a woman who understood him and he felt the thrill of her acceptance. She did not demand more than he was able to give. If anything, she was the one to put restrictions on their relationship. He adored her for not trying to change him or lasso him into a long-term relationship.

He'd never met anyone quite like her before. She was a paradox. At once down-to-earth and steadfast but with a sexy playful streak that never failed to catch him off guard.

And he loved her dichotomy. She kept him guessing.

She reached across the console between the seats and touched his hand. ''Are you ready for a night to remember?'' Her low, husky voice sent a flashback of heat rolling through his system.

''Are you kidding? I'm up for anything. Always.''

Her throaty chuckle sent goose bumps flying up his arms. ''Yes,'' she said. ''Yes, you are.''

Taking his eyes off the road for a whisper of a second, he pinned her with a stare. She licked her lips and they gleamed wetly in the darkness.

A jolt of awareness caught him by the short hairs. God, she'd never been so desirable as she was at this moment.

He stepped on the accelerator and the Ferrari leaped forward, his mind awash in testosterone, his body hard, hot and ready for her. When they arrived at the B and B, he hopped from the car and rushed over to the passenger side to help her out.

She tossed her head and peered up into his face. Her hair was windblown from the convertible, her dress rumpled from all that dancing, her eyes ablaze with hedonistic purpose. She looked wild and wanton and totally sexy.

This was what he'd wanted from the moment he'd spied her in the window of Wickedly Wonderful. This jolt, this drive, this live spark of sexual heat.

A turbocharged affair with a rebellious woman and nothing more.

Tonight would be the culmination of his dreams.

He struggled to keep his hand from shaking as he took her elbow and guided her into the B and B. His heart thundered, rapping against his rib cage like an electrical storm.

They climbed the creaky stairs to their bedroom, the muted lighting from the wall sconces illuminating their way. Eden's hands were all over him. Touching his back, reaching up to stroke his chin, skipping along his knuckles.

But once they were inside their room and the door had closed behind them, Eden turned hesitant. She pulled her hand from his and moved away from him, away from the bed looming out from the wall in suggestive invitation.

He sensed the shift in her mood but could not ascertain why, in a matter of seconds, she'd gone from red-hot to reticent.

He stared deeply into her misty blue eyes and spotted passion mixed with uneasiness. This reaction was new. What was different?

The answer came to him. Ah. She had no costume to hide behind. No three-hundred-dollar-a-night-call-girl/ cheerleader-from-the-wrong-side-of-the-tracks/ dominatrix-business-woman persona to hide behind.

It was just the two of them alone in a bedroom. No pretenses, no charades, no provocative scenarios.

That's what had her rattled.

Alec took a step toward her.

She waltzed back.

He came forward.

Eden sidestepped, but he went with her, literally

forcing her into the corner until her butt was pressed against the window ledge and she had nowhere else to go. By intentionally invading her personal space, he was heightening both the tension and her arousal.

Eden gulped, swallowing back her fears. This was it. The moment they'd been building up to for the past four weeks. The moment when she finally revealed to him her secret.

What would he do? she fretted. Would he, like Josh, flee in disgust?

What if...

Stop it, she chided herself and reached for the worry stone in her pocket. She rubbed the stone's smooth, comforting surface with her thumb and felt her worries abate. Alec wasn't Josh. He was impulsive, yes, and spontaneous and unpredictable.

But he was also kind and considerate and endearingly vulnerable in his own way. Why else would the man jump out of perfectly good airplanes and snowboard down steep mountains and take all manner of daredevil risks if he wasn't trying to compensate for something? Why else was he so terrified of commitment?

He used activities and plans and even sex as a buffer against pain and suffering.

Even though she could not fully verbalize why, Eden understood this about him. And because she understood Alec and recognized his vulnerability she felt safe with him. She knew he would never intentionally hurt her.

That thought gave her the courage to reach for the zipper on her dress.

"Let me," Alec commanded, his voice rough and demanding.

Trembling, she turned and presented her back to him. She lifted the hair off the nape of her neck and heard his raspy intake of breath. A second later, she felt his hot, moist lips tickle her collarbone.

When he grasped her shoulders with both his hands, she trembled and arched her back against his body. Her butt came into direct contact with his pelvis.

His groan circled the room and came to rest in her ears, the erotic sound echoing deep within her. Eden's pulse skipped.

This was different. Tonight was different. The mood, the tone, the way he touched her—all different. It was more intimate, the sweep of his mouth more detailed, the wistful longing inside her more bittersweet.

God, she was wet and hot and ready for him.

He inched the zipper down with his teeth, his fingers stroked a gentle path over the skin he bared. She shivered and moaned softly.

"I'm going to make love to you all night long," he murmured. "Tonight is all about you. First, I'm going to love you with my hands. Then, I'm going to love you with my mouth."

"And then?" she whispered, her voice as tight and thin as a guitar string.

"And then I'm going to love you with my body.

I'm going to make you come again and again and again.''

She hissed in her breath. His fingers trailed her bare back down to her bra. Smoothly he unhooked it and then gently turned her around to face him.

"Look at me," he commanded.

Helplessly Eden raised her head even though she was scared out of her wits. Would this evening end in exquisite pleasure or would he soon be on his way out the door?

But the expression in his warm gray eyes vanquished all her fears. At least temporarily. His heated gaze caressed her, sent hot daggers of anticipation darting through her groin.

It was as if he couldn't get enough of peering deeply into her eyes. Eden's heart strummed with hope. He made her feel cherished and cared for and utterly secure. It was a strange emotion to feel with a gadabout playboy who could have his pick of any woman, but there it was. The calm, settled sense that she could trust this man not to turn away from her because her body was less than cover-model perfect.

"I want to see you naked."

"Okay."

"All of you." He never once lowered his eyes.

She nodded.

"In the light."

"Yes." She barely managed to force the word past her lips.

He stepped over and switched on the bedside lamp, bathing the room in bright light. Eden moistened her lips and quelled the urge to flee. He returned to stand before her.

"I want to see those beautiful breasts." As Alec spoke, he eased her dress over her shoulders, taking the straps of her bra down with the soft, silky material.

She closed her eyes briefly, gathered her courage. She could do this. She would do this.

He stroked her skin. "I want to see every inch of you. I've been at a disadvantage this whole time. You've kept yourself hidden, teasing me with your sexy games, but this is our last night together. No more games, Eden. No more toys. No more pretending. It's just you and me and that big soft bed over there."

He pressed her back flush against the wall. Her dress was pulled to her waist and her bra slipped unnoticed to the floor. Alec leaned down and nibbled one of her nipples that had stiffened at the brush of his knuckles.

A sigh of pleasure slipped past her lips.

"Mustn't play favorites," he murmured, moving to ensnare the other nipple between his teeth.

The hot glide of his mouth drove her to distraction. She couldn't think of anything except how good it felt to have his wet tongue strumming over the beaded bud.

He licked and tasted and sucked. Her internal hunger for him escalated to a throbbing ache.

She arched her pelvis against him. He wrapped one

hand around her waist while the other hand slowly inched her dress down over her hips.

Soon. Soon now he would discover her scar.

Fresh worry filtered through her as his tongue inched from her breasts down her rib cage to her flat smooth belly.

He stopped what he was doing, straightened and took a step back. His gaze immediately sought hers. "You're trembling."

"Am I?" A hard shudder passed through her.

He cupped her cheek in his palm, "Sweetheart, are you all right?"

Tears welled up tight in her throat and she couldn't answer.

"Have I done something to hurt you? Scare you?"

"No."

"What is it then?"

She shook her head.

"Do you want to stop?" He looked confused.

"No," she whispered desperately. That was the last thing she wanted.

Do it. Show him. Now is the time.

"What's the matter, Eden? It's okay. You can say anything to me."

His words gave her permission and the look in his eyes gave her faith. With her heart slamming against her ears loud as cannon fire, she hooked her thumbs into the waistband of her satin tap pants and pushed them down along with the folded material of the dress draped around her hips.

Courageously she stood before him, totally exposed

in the bright glow of lamplight. She held her breath and raised her head to gauge his initial gut reaction.

His eyes widened at the sight of her scar. The air rattled through his lungs with an audible rasp. The expression on his face was one of tender concern, not revulsion or horror.

She prepared herself for a barrage of questions about the scars, but he took her completely by surprise.

"So this is what you've been hiding from me." He shook his head and clicked his tongue.

"You're not grossed out?" she whispered.

"Did you really think it would matter? Good Lord, woman, what you must think of me."

"It happened before. With another guy."

"Well, that guy was an asshole. And I'm not him."

She was so overcome by his acceptance that she simply couldn't speak.

"You're beautiful, Eden Montgomery, inside and out and no scar is going to obscure that fact." He went down on his knees, kneeling before her and gently pressed his lips to her scars to prove his point.

The tears that had blocked her throat flooded into her eyes. Fat crocodile drops rolled down her cheeks and plopped onto the top of his head. She felt relieved and brave and free.

She'd dared, at long last, to reveal herself to him and Alec hadn't disappointed her. She'd faced her fears and he'd rewarded her with deeper sexual intimacy than anything she'd ever experienced.

Simply put, she felt like the queen of the world.

No matter what happened from this moment on, she would cherish the precious gift he'd just given her.

It was enough.

Alec clasped her tightly around the waist, pulled her pelvis flush against his face. The scratch of his beard stubble against the tender flesh of her wound was at once erotic and unfamiliar.

He ran his tongue along the edges of the scar, branding her with his tongue. He kissed her naked muff once, twice, three times and then without another word, got to his feet, lifted her into his arms and carried her like a princess on her wedding night into his bed.

13

HER BODY WAS a wonderland.

Lush, ripe, rounded. A playground of endless delights.

After stripping off his clothes and rolling on a condom, reverentially, Alec climbed into bed beside Eden. He buried his face in her hair, inhaled deeply and sank into pure bliss.

For the longest time, he simply explored.

He could not get enough of looking at her or tasting her or skimming his hands over her curves. Her lack of hair down there fascinated him and the raw pink edges of her scars evoked a tenderness deep inside him that defied explanation.

His chest ached with the thought of all she'd suffered. It literally hurt him to imagine what she'd been through. More than anything he wanted to be the one to whisk away her pain and transport her to a place of pure, unadulterated pleasure.

Over the course of the past month, she'd given him so much delight; it was his turn to repay the favor. He knew to be gentle with her. When he trailed his kisses down her torso to tickle her warm, soft belly, he lingered a moment giving her time to adjust, before moving downward into tender territory.

Eden tensed.

"It's okay, babe," he crooned, and rested his cheek against her pelvis.

He stroked her until she relaxed. Everything melted away. His universe narrowed to this one spectacular moment, this one spectacular woman, this wondrous world all safe and clean and female.

She curled her fingers into his hair and cooed softly whenever he did something that pleased her. He caressed her with his tongue, slowly and thoroughly heating her damaged skin. She raised her hips off the bed and a soft whimpering noise escaped her lips.

He lifted his head to look at her.

"More," she whispered, and parted her legs. "More."

Sweet heaven, she was ready.

He shifted around, positioning himself between those lovely thighs. He gazed in wonder at the full view of her—so smooth and round and pink and bare.

Cautiously, so as not to hurt her, Alec dipped his head to part her swollen cleft and languidly swept his tongue across her most private spot.

Her taste was incredible. Sweet and yet slightly salty. Earthy and womanly and robust.

"Oh Alec, yes," she hissed through clenched teeth. "Yes."

"Tell me more," he said. "Tell me exactly how you like it."

"Firmer, faster."

He complied, excited that she'd overcome her earlier hesitation and let herself go. Soon she was describing every detail, telling him precisely what felt good and what did not.

Pride expanded his chest. He felt damned privileged he was with her and awestruck she'd allowed him in on her very personal secret.

Then Eden was beyond speech and Alec found himself working only with silent commands: a writhe, sharp intake of breath, fingernails biting into his shoulder.

He painstakingly searched out her erogenous zones, savoring every secret spot, kissing and nibbling and licking her glistening feminine pinkness. He captured her straining nub between his lips and gently probed it with his hungry tongue when suddenly, violently her hips arched high, bucking them both into the air.

From deep inside Eden came a cross between a startled scream and a desperate groan. The sound echoed off the plaster walls.

Flailing her head from side to side, she grasped his hair, clasping him fast between her thighs and frantically raking her heels across his back. He shoved deep, pushing her to the top and ruthlessly holding her orgasm at bay while torturing her with his tongue, letting her teeter on the edge.

Again and again, he teased. Pushing her hard, then backing off.

She moaned and grunted and cried and clawed at his hair.

Then she gave one loud long gasp and it was over.

She lay still against the mattress, mewling softly, her breasts heaving.

Out of breath and feeling smug, Alec rolled over and collapsed onto the covers beside her, listening to his body throb. So much blood was diverted to his solid steel erection, he couldn't stop smiling. He reached over, took Eden's hand and squeezed it.

She squeezed back. His smile widened and he closed his eyes.

He had never heard a woman make the kind of uninhibited noise she had just uttered and he couldn't get over the fact he'd been the cause of it.

A moment longer of mutual heavy breathing and then Eden moved over to kneel between his legs. His eyes flew open and he saw an irregular splash of strawberry covering her chest, glowing hot and vivid against the creamy white of her skin.

Her face was radiant. She tucked a strand of chestnut hair behind one ear and slanted him a coy glance. The bright color crept up her throat to encompass even her chin. A woman could fake an orgasm, but she couldn't fake that sexual blush. Alec realized with a start that she was proudly showing him her scarlet flush.

He'd never felt so self-satisfied.

But she only allowed him a moment to bask in his macho glory. Reaching down, she gently squeezed his cock.

"Don't," he gave a strangled cry. "Too soon."

"Are you about to come?" she whispered.

He nodded.

She tweaked the head of his penis.

He groaned.

She giggled, jumped up and before she spun away, threw him a daring look over her shoulder that said *catch me if you can.*

But he could tell from her squeal of laughter that he was quicker than she anticipated. He scrambled to his knees and snagged her around the waist before she cleared the floor. With his face pressed against the small of her back, he wrestled her back down upon the bed.

He was harder than he'd ever been. One wrong move and it was all over. He was hard and hot and horny.

Horny, hell. Who was he kidding? He was literally on fire with need.

Gently he urged her onto her hands and knees, every bone, every muscle, every cell in his bone screamed for release as he pushed her head down against a pillow and slid his knees between hers from behind, his manhood jutting out like a tall soldier, wedging upright in the soft valley of her beautiful female behind.

She made a strangled noise, fought to raise her head and trashed her hips against him. He paused to make sure he hadn't played too rough. He was just about to let her go when the tip of his cock slipped down between her legs and pressed eagerly against the damp opening of her sheath.

Alec froze.

Eden froze.

Then, with a high-pitched, almost pitiful mew, she dropped her head—her dark hair spilling luxuriously across the white pillowcase—and swayed her back like a cat enticing a mate, rolled her luscious bottom at him in a posture both supplicant and demanding.

For a blink in time, he didn't move. He simply knelt there behind her, amazed at the feelings zipping through him. Pride and awe and greed and need. Tenderness and recklessness and adoration and glee.

He remained posed like that, pressing against her opening. She succumbed to his heaviness only ever so slightly, her warmth expanding over the head of him with agonizing slowness as he skimmed his fingers around her bottom and up her spine, chasing the goose bumps racing to the nape of her neck while she rolled her head, inhaling and exhaling through clenched teeth with a throaty, feral rasp.

He held his breath and caressed her shoulders, her back, her hips and then the tender area of her scarred thighs. It was all he could do to keep from impaling her with one famished thrust. But he forced himself to wait, to savor the moment.

To relish in her passion.

He swallowed shallow gulps of air as he held himself back. Slowly she dilated against his masculine pressure. Millimeter by excruciating millimeter, he entered her, the slow, deliberate motions sending novel waves of pleasure-pain scorching through his tortured genitals.

Then all at once, he was embedded within her, curved and stone hard, filling her up.

Yieldingly she stretched for him while at the same time firmly enveloping him in her wet heat. She was snug and tight against his entire length.

He paused again at that point, still anxious to drag it out as long as possible, her rich, feminine scent reaching up to him, caressing him with piquant fingers. He inhaled her sex and the world spun away. He was fuzzy-headed and consumed by the moment and his sweet, loving woman.

But without warning she took over, constricting herself around him, rhythmically gripping and squeezing his erection.

What power she possessed.

She looked back at him then, through the curtain of her hair and her fevered eyes locked onto his. Eyes pleading yet giving. Eyes glistening with lust, pure and unashamed.

A knot of emotion clogged his chest when he realized that because of him, she'd thrown off her embarrassment over her scars. She opened herself up to him, embracing him with an astonishing vitality.

How brave she was. How daring.

Admiration for her surged, became twins with his desire. She was one hell of a woman and he would never, ever forget her.

He sank his fingers into her hips and she pushed back against him, her hunger, her demand as unmistakable as his own.

What he felt was better than any adrenaline rush from extreme sports. The power, the pleasure, the glory swept him away in an unstoppable tide of sensation.

He was Hercules, strong and invincible, bellowing in the storm atop Mount Olympus as lightning burned his thighs and thunder rumbled low from his loins, beckoning forth the hot torrential release that rushed and streamed from Alec into his woman, his lady, his goddess, who raged with him. Their voices rejoiced in their union while she hungrily consumed his spasms, evoking the next and the next and the next.

And the next.

When it was over, they lay cuddled together in a panting, twisted heap, inebriated by the afterglow. He cradled her against his arm and softly kissed her forehead. She murmured and burrowed against his chest.

They were damp with sweat. Their backs and bellies and thighs were slick with the moisture of sex. He rubbed his beard stubble against her skin and she giggled, the bubbly sound as intoxicating as champagne.

He drifted on a cloud of happiness, spent and sated. Everything was perfect.

In a matter of minutes Eden was sound asleep, her gentle breathing music to his ears. He delighted in the weight of her head against his shoulder, the wonderful scent of her in his nostrils. Alec realized it had been a very long time since he had been this happy.

He dozed for a while but soon felt her warm lips nibbling at his collarbone.

"Can we go again?" she whispered, her hand

stroking his manhood, coaxing his sleeping warrior back to the battlefield.

"So soon?"

"It's our last night together," she reminded him. "We've got no time for sleep."

Although he was tired and sore, his bones liquid, he rose to the occasion.

Literally.

Seemingly from out of nowhere, Eden produced a fresh condom, cupped his balls in her palm and playfully capped his erection.

He couldn't believe he was so hot and ready for her again so soon after that last massive explosion, but she had an unerring talent for knowing just where to touch, just how to turn him into a bundle of throbbing testosterone.

But in spite of the wildness marching through his veins, this time he wanted something slow and quiet. He flipped her onto her back and positioned himself above her, pinning her to the bed.

They were eye to eye, her breath warm against his chin. He propped his weight on his forearms, his pounding manhood pressed against her soft belly. They lay pelvis to pelvis, skin to skin, the smoothness of her breasts flush against his hard chest. It was an exhilarating and erotic moment. Their skin seared together, instant heat spreading from him to her and her to him.

Slowly he entered her willing body and she uttered a happy sigh. The sound touched him.

Compelled by a force he could not explain, Alec

stopped moving inside her. He cupped her cheeks in his palms and stared and stared and stared at her. Past the thickly lashed eyes, over the blue iris and into her pupils.

He tumbled down, down, down into the glorious abyss of Eden's pure essence. He kissed her deeply, soulfully, without ever closing his eyes. She kept her eyes open, too, and that's when he felt something dangerous slip inside his heart.

A treacherous emotion he did not dare name but had spent his entire adulthood avoiding, blooming inside his chest, crowding his heart, tightening his lungs, clogging his throat. This kind of emotional intimacy did not fit into his plans. Never had, never would.

The desperate urge to flee encompassed him. He'd never bargained for this feeling. Didn't want anything to do with the repercussions.

It was at that moment Alec Ramsey knew he was in serious trouble.

HER SCARS DIDN'T REPULSE HIM.

Eden couldn't get over the fact that her disfigurement hadn't slowed Alec's ardor one whit. Beneath his expert hands, all her doubts and fears vanished as she gave herself up to the ultimate in physical intimacy.

She gazed over at him. He slept peacefully on his back, one arm flung over his head. His gentle snores caused a flutter in her stomach. She smiled to herself. She was a lucky, lucky woman.

His ready acceptance had freed her. He had acted as if the scars were simply a part of her, like the color of her eyes or the texture of her hair. His tender touch, quirky smile and sexy wink opened the door to a big wide world of sensation and, for that, she would be forever grateful.

Tonight she'd let herself go with stormy abandon, holding nothing back, indulging herself completely. She'd faced her greatest fear and won. Courage had led to the physical intimacy she craved. He'd given her back the self-esteem Josh had stolen away.

Alec was the perfect love mentor. She had chosen wisely.

Now all that remained was saying goodbye.

Unexpected emotion stabbed her chest and she bit down on her bottom lip. She didn't want to say goodbye to him, which was exactly why she must. She'd put a limit on their affair and she'd been unbending every time he'd asked her to break the rules. She'd feared she would fall in love with him if she allowed their sexual exploration to go on too long. And from the looks of things she'd stopped just in the nick of time.

Another weekend with him and she might not have had the courage to say goodbye.

Do you have the courage now? The pesky question circled her brain, echoing annoyingly.

Yes. She wasn't in love with him.

Yet.

Just because she couldn't seem to think about anything else but Alec didn't mean she was in love. Obsessed with sex, maybe, but how could she be in love with a man who willingly admitted he was not the marrying kind?

And even though she had not gone into this relationship looking for a long-term commitment, Eden knew that eventually she wanted what most people wanted. True love. She wanted a husband, a home, a family to call her own.

Alec had simply been a means to an end. The vehicle that had taken her from fearful to courageous. Because of him, she could finally leave behind the pain of the fire. They'd entered into this mutually beneficial agreement fully aware of the stipulations and limitations. Now was not the time for second-guessing.

As of tomorrow, when they returned to the city, the affair was officially over. She refused to second-guess her decision. She had grown and changed. A bright future beckoned.

A future without Alec.

Something painful twisted in her chest, but she closed her eyes and ignored the emotion.

You're just sorry to be losing out on all that great sex, she told herself. *It's nothing more than that.*

So why did she yearn for more?

Because she was greedy. Greedy for more kisses, more caresses, more tender looks. Because she wanted to keep having screaming orgasms with him. Because she liked the way it felt curled up beside him.

What was the matter with her? She was an adult.

She'd gone into this thing with her eyes open. Alec had given her the wonderful gift of her own sexuality; she simply refused to ruin what they'd shared by expecting anything more.

As long as he didn't plead with her to continue their relationship, she could handle saying goodbye.

But what if he did?

ALEC WOKE BEFORE EDEN. He eased his arm out from under her head to slip from the bed. He hurried into the bathroom and climbed into the shower. He intended to be fully clothed when he faced her again. If she reached for him, kissed him, or even looked into his eyes, he knew he would make love to her one last time.

And that was a risk he simply couldn't take.

When they'd made love for the fourth time in the wee hours of the morning, he had experienced a rush of powerful emotions. Emotions he was not prepared to deal with.

The hot water sluiced over his body. He wished it could wash away the strange feelings swishing inside of him. Feelings perilously close to love.

He couldn't be in love with Eden. No way, no how. He didn't fall in love. He was Alec Ramsey, editor in chief of *Single Guy*. His whole life, his entire career, his very reputation was founded on the premise that he remain a swinging bachelor.

So why was it that every time he closed his eyes, he kept seeing Eden wearing his ring? Why, despite every effort to stop the mental pictures, did he visualize her pregnant with his baby? Why dammit, did he keep imagining a house in Connecticut?

The persistent imagery scared him straight to his marrow.

It's just the hot sex, dude. You've never experienced such great bedroom antics with anyone else and you've mistaken it for love. That's all it is. Don't freak. Don't read anything more into this.

Right. Stunningly great sex, not love. That was the ticket. He was panicking for nothing.

Besides, Eden had made it clear enough she wasn't interested in anything but a short-term fling. He'd gotten what he'd wanted. A wickedly wonderful affair with a naughty woman.

But while the affair had brought the physical release he'd sought, it had not given him what he'd needed most—renewed faith in his carefree single lifestyle.

In fact, his time with Eden had only compounded his restless dissatisfaction and stoked his desire for something more meaningful than parties and good times and a bevy of beautiful women on his arm.

It was her burn scars, he analyzed. That's what made her different from the others. That's why he felt such tenderness for her. Her vulnerability touched him in a way no one else ever had. Sympathy was what he was feeling for her. Sympathy and admiration and respect.

Not love.

As long as he kept reminding himself of that, he'd
be okay.

Right?

"THESE PAST FOUR WEEKS have been really special
for me," Eden said as Alec guided his Ferrari down
the ribbon of highway, headed for Manhattan on Sun-
day afternoon. "I just thought you should know
that."

He glanced over at her and his gut torqued. She
looked so beautiful sitting there in a cream-colored
sweater and black leather pants, her head tilted in that
endearing way of hers, a smile lifting the corner of
her small but full lips.

This past month had been damned special for him,
too, but he wasn't about to admit it. If he named the
emotion knotting his chest, he feared deepening the
intimacy between them and laying himself open to
the pain of loneliness that he'd spent a lifetime struggling to deny.

Nope, best to ignore the feelings warring inside
him and pretend everything was fine. He had a busy
life. Activities crowded his plate. The magazine kept
him hopping. He had loads of friends. What did he
have to be lonely about?

"You helped me a lot, whether you know it or
not," she continued.

"Helped you?" He glued his eyes to the road. For
no good reason, his pulse hammered in his ears. "I
didn't do anything."

"Oh, yes, you did," she murmured. The sound of
her soft, homey voice curled around him like an elec-

tric blanket switched on high—warm and inviting. "You restored my self-esteem."

"Who? Me?"

"I've got a confession to make."

His body tensed and he clenched his jaw. What was she going to say?

"Eden," he said a little too brusquely. He felt bad for sounding rude, but he was hoping to head off true confessions. "This is the last time we'll see each other. There's no need to reveal any secrets we might have been keeping from each other."

"It's just something I thought you should know." She sounded hurt.

Ah, dammit. The last thing he wanted was to hurt her. Hell, that's why he'd chosen her for this affair, because in the beginning she'd been as adamant as he that this was only about sex and nothing else.

He had the strangest urge to turn on the radio or start talking about quantum physics or even stick his fingers in his ears and hum so loudly he couldn't hear her. Instead, he pressed down on the gas, eager to get back to the city as soon as possible. The sooner they went their separate ways the sooner he could shake off this odd melancholy dogging him.

What in the hell are you so afraid of, Ramsey?

She turned her face away from him and her shoulders slumped. He felt like a complete and utter jerk.

"Okay," he said, tamping down his guilt. "Go ahead. If you'd like to get something off your chest, I'm listening."

She hesitated for a long moment. "Nah, you're right. What's the point?"

Alec reached across the seat and squeezed her hand. Just touching her sent a jolt of pleasure mingled with sadness zinging through his veins. "Come on, I want to hear this."

Silence.

"What do you have to tell me?" he encouraged while at the same moment praying that she wasn't going to confess that she'd fallen in love with him.

"You're the first lover I've had since the...er, the..." she stammered.

"Since you got burned," he said softly.

God, what was the matter with him? Why was he going all gooey and marshmallowy inside? He wasn't a sensitive, touchy-feely kind of guy.

"Yes. I haven't made love to anyone since the fire and only one man before that. I feel guilty because I led you to believe that I was this sexually liberated woman who can handle casual sex, when nothing could be further from the truth."

Uh-oh! What was she saying?

"If you hadn't given me the worry stone I don't think I would have been able to go through with this. But when you sent me the stone, it was like you could read my mind. Like you knew exactly what I needed in order to gather my courage."

"Babe," he said, struggling to sound laid-back and belying the anxiety gripping him. "I was in the bed with you, believe me, you *are* one red-hot lady. Worry stone or not."

"But it's all pretend. I read books and talked to my friend Jayne. I watched instructional videos and practiced on fruit."

"Practiced on fruit?" He chuckled more to break the tension than anything else. Fact was, he found it pretty endearing that she'd gone to such efforts in order to learn how to please him.

"Don't laugh at me."

"I'm not laughing at you, honest."

"I'm trying to confess to you."

"I'm listening."

"You're grinning."

"I can listen and grin at the same time."

"I'm not a love-'em-and-leave-'em sort of gal. I'm not into the freewheeling bachelorette lifestyle. I want to get married someday. I want to have kids. I'm not like you, Alec. If I look into the future and see myself forever single, I feel lonely, not emancipated."

"So you lied to me?" He zipped around a slow-moving tractor-trailer rig. He was driving too fast and he knew it but this sensation of claustrophobia had him feeling that if he dared slow down he'd get trapped in Connecticut forever.

"I'm sorry. I didn't lie, at least not intentionally. You assumed I was a wild woman because of my profession and I let you believe it. The way you looked at me made me feel wild and I liked it. And I wanted a casual fling. I wanted to sow my oats. All I'm trying to say is thank you for being the one I sowed them with. That's all."

"That's it?"

He felt strangely used. She'd gotten what she wanted and now she was tossing him aside.

But this was a good thing, right? He'd been worrying that she might be falling in love with him. He should be relieved, not miffed at her deception.

"Thank you, Alec. Thank you for giving me back the sexuality I lost after the fire."

"You're welcome," he said hoarsely, because he did not know what else to say.

14

ALEC LEFT HER on the sidewalk outside Wickedly Wonderful without a backward glance. He had broken every speed limit getting her back to Manhattan. It was as if he couldn't dump her fast enough.

Eden watched the Ferrari speed away. Turning, she inserted her key into the lock and let herself into the boutique.

You shouldn't have confessed your sexual inexperience.

But he'd been acting weird before then. He'd gotten out of bed before she awoke. He'd showered and dressed while she still slept. He hadn't spoken much and when she'd teasingly tried to undress him for one last mattress wrestle before checkout, he'd gently turned her down. He'd been subdued and he'd had trouble making eye contact with her. When she'd made a few jokes, he hadn't laughed.

Listlessly she dropped her suitcase and purse on the counter and sank into the chair beside the phone. The message light blinked. Sighing, she dropped her head into her hands and told herself she was *not* going to cry.

The silly fear she'd harbored that Alec might plead

with her to continue their affair vanished completely. What had changed? Why had he gone from urging her to extend their time together to kicking her out of his car as quickly as possible?

She searched for an explanation. What had happened to the man she had shared so much with the night before? Had she said something untoward, done something to embarrass him? What had changed?

The answer hit her like a hard boot to the head.

She recalled daringly guiding his hand to her thigh this morning. That's when the odd expression had come over his face, that's when he'd pulled back, told her they didn't have time for another romp.

Bile rose in her throat.

He'd covered up his distaste pretty well last night, but obviously he hadn't wanted to touch her scar again in the light of day after his passion had worn off. And why should he? He could have his pick of women, why would he want to saddle himself with someone who was less than perfect?

Face facts, Eden. You're damaged goods. Ultimately, even a sexual connoisseur like Alec wasn't able to look past her flaws. How else could she explain his abrupt change in behavior?

The old doubts she thought she'd vanquished spilled into her mind, gnawing and gnashing on her. She reached into her pocket to finger the worry stone, but for once the rock did nothing to allay her fears.

Stop it! You've come too far to sink this low again, she chided herself.

Feeling sadder but wiser, she leaned over and depressed the message button on the answering machine. Anything to take her mind off Alec.

"Eden? This is Tori Drake," the voice of the Spice-Up-Your-Love-Life representative spun off the tape and filled the room.

Eden tensed and caught her breath. Had they liked the new basket or was she about to lose her biggest account?

"I'm calling to tell you congratulations are in order. The executives *loved* your new basket design. You did a superb job. Not only are we renewing your contract, but we're also upping the order. Call me on Monday. Have a nice weekend."

Eden exhaled sharply. She should have been over-the-moon-elated. She had bested her creative slump, she'd had terrific sex with Alec and she'd discovered so much about herself in the process. She should be happy, excited, overjoyed.

But instead she felt hollow, empty, sad. Even though she'd convinced herself that all she wanted was to play the bad girl and indulge in a four-week fling, she realized that was not what she wanted at all.

Because in that moment, she realized what was wrong.

In spite of her best intentions to the contrary, she'd made the cardinal mistake of falling in love with Alec Ramsey.

"I'VE GOT SOMETHING important to tell you," Uncle Mac yelled, as they stood poised on the face of the hard, cold granite cliff of Kjerag, Norway. A glacier wind whipped their hair about their faces. "And this is difficult for me to admit."

"What is it?" Alec shouted, barely able to hear above the wind. He, Mac and their guide, Yuri, had just endured a twenty-eight-hundred-foot climb with parachutes strapped to their backs. The rugged beauty of the mountain landscape stretched endless before them.

It was two weeks after Randy's wedding and Alec hadn't been able to stop thinking about Eden. When Mac had sauntered into his office two days before and suggested another parachute jump off Kjerag, he'd leaped at the chance.

Something, anything to erase Eden from his mind. A spontaneous trip to throw himself headlong off a cliff in Norway seemed exactly what he needed. An exciting thrill ride to get his blood pumping again.

Alec looked at his uncle. Why had Mac picked this moment to start a serious conversation?

Mac flashed him a toothy grin, took off on a running exit and just as he bolted off the overhang and into the void below, he hollered, "Sophie and I are getting married."

Alec blinked and shook his head, certain he must have heard wrong. He watched Mac's canopy open. His uncle glided gracefully down to the earth.

Yuri gave him the thumbs-up. "Get it on!"

Alec stared into the abyss, hovering on the edge, Mac's statement echoing in his head. *Sophie and I are getting married.*

Never, ever in a million years had he expected his uncle to utter those words.

"Rock and roll, dude!" Yuri said, the American slang sounding comical coming from his Norwegian lips.

Alec looked straight out and then slightly up to pick a point to focus on during his exit. He took a deep breath to empty his mind of Mac's strange declaration and tilted his body forward. His feet had not yet left solid ground but the leap had already begun. He was committed now and there was no going back.

He pushed off vigorously at a forty-five-degree angle as his body departed the ledge.

"Yipee-kay-yi-yay!" Yuri called after him.

The Norwegian had been watching too many Hollywood movies.

Seconds into the jump Alec knew his exit had been perfect. The wind screamed in his ears. He maintained a hard arch for the first three or four seconds before lengthening his legs and easing his arms back into track position.

The free fall should have been exhilarating. He was tumbling headlong into nothingness, but instead of euphoria, he felt bizarrely empty, his senses dulled.

It was fun, yes.

But not as much fun as spending time with Eden.

The cliffs whizzed by, magnificent in their frozen glory.

But not as magnificent as the glow of Eden's face in candlelight.

The sight of the ground rising up to meet him was mind-blowing.

But not nearly as mind-blowing as the picture of Eden flipping over the hourglass before positioning herself between his naked thighs.

At fifteen seconds, he deployed his chute. The canopy exploded out behind him—his safety net that he had faith in one hundred percent.

Why couldn't he have that much faith in his feelings for Eden?

His breath came in short, raspy gasps, not from the megarush of the free fall but rather from the memory of Eden and all the wonderful things they'd shared.

He found himself coming straight down, nice and easy, with virtually no forward speed. The perfect landing. Everything had turned out fine.

Mac joined him, slapped him on the back. "Awesome stuff, eh. God, I've never felt so alive. Except of course, when I'm with Sophie."

"Did I hear you right?" Alec demanded, unbuckling his harness. "Before you jumped, did you say you and Sophie were getting married?"

Mac had the good grace to blush. "I did."

"The lifelong bachelor, getting hitched?"

"Yep. I finally decided to grow up."

Perplexed, Alec could only stare. "But what brought all this on? Why now? Why Sophie?"

Mac cleared his throat. "I guess you could say my priorities have been rearranged."

"Since when?" Alec frowned. For the course of his entire life he'd idealized Uncle Mac, had sought to emulate him, had been honored to follow in his footsteps. Mac couldn't have surprised him more if he'd announced he'd just had a sex change operation.

"Remember when I came back from Fiji early?"

"Yes."

"It was because I'd been feeling poorly."

"You were sick and you didn't tell me?"

"I couldn't talk about it. I wasn't ready to face my mortality."

"Your mortality?"

"Let's go sit in the Jeep, get out of this wind, share a thermos of coffee."

Alec nodded and followed his uncle to the Jeep parked at the base of the mountain. They crowded into the front seat. Mac started the engine and turned on the heater.

"Okay. Spill," Alec said, rubbing his chapped hands together to warm them.

"When you hear the word 'cancer' applied to you it sort of puts things in perspective."

"Cancer?" Alec felt the blood drain from his face. His beloved uncle, the man who'd been a father to him ever since his own father died, was stricken with cancer?

"The doctors thought it was malignant. They did a biopsy and the tumor turned out to be benign. But those weeks while I waited for the biopsy to be scheduled were excruciating and I was forced to do a lot of soul-searching."

"So you're getting married now because you were scared?"

Mac shook his head. ''I'm getting married because I finally admitted to myself that I love Sophie. She's been my rock. Throughout this whole ordeal she's been right by my side. I'm embarrassed to think of the cavalier way I've treated her over the years, coming in and out of her life on my own whims. I was determined to do things my way. Lucky for me, she forgave me for being such a jerk.''

''But all those years, you said marriage was a straitjacket.'' Alec shook his head, still unable to comprehend what his uncle was telling him. ''You said a predictable life was worse than death.''

''I was wrong.''

Stunned, Alec took the thermos of coffee that Mac held out to him. Everything he'd ever believed in was turned topsy-turvy. He felt angry and confused and hurt and relieved.

Yes, relieved. Because of Mac's confession, maybe he too could admit that he'd been wrong.

He had no trouble releasing control when it came to daredevil stunts. He relished the thrilling experiences. He loved testing his body's limits.

So why did he have such resistance to mental risks? Why did emotional intimacy scare the pants off him? How come he could commit to hurling his body through space but he could not manage to admit he needed something more?

''WHAT DO YOU MEAN it's over?'' Jayne Lockerbee bit down on her thumb and trailed Eden through the store as she put together the latest shipment for Spice-Up-Your-Love-Life Cruises.

"Hmm?" Distracted, Eden barely glanced up from the Farmer's Frisky Daughter theme basket.

"You two looked so adorable together at Jill and Randy's wedding. I can't believe you broke up."

Eden stopped immediately. Although two weeks had gone by since the last time she'd made love to Alec, her body still throbbed with the memories they'd made together.

After having her imagination kindled to a full roaring blaze by his incredible caresses it had been hard going back to her quiet life. She'd taken all that excess energy and channeled it into her work. Business was booming and that's the way she wanted it. If she kept busy, she was less likely to get depressed over how things had gone with Alec.

She wondered how long it would take her to get over him. A month? Two? Three?

What if she never got over him? What if she spent the rest of her life mooning over an unobtainable man?

Stop it right there, Eden Montgomery, she chided herself. *No more worst-case scenarios. By taking a chance, you've learned you can live through the worst and survive. No more feeling sorry for yourself.* If nothing else, the pain of losing Alec was worth that lesson.

"Alec and I were never together. I told you from the beginning this thing between us was just a sexual adventure. It was never meant to be anything more."

"I don't know about that. If you work sexual magic on a man, he tends to fall in love with you. That's how I snagged Roger. It wasn't my cooking, believe me."

"Jayne!"

"It's the truth."

"Well, I tried every trick you taught me and Alec didn't fall in love with me."

"How do you know?"

"For one thing, he's married to that friggin' magazine."

"Did he tell you he didn't want to see you again?"

"He didn't have to." Just the recollection of how Alec had sped away, leaving her on the curb outside Wickedly Wonderful caused the pain to rise up inside her fresh and raw.

"So it really is over."

"Ka-put. Finished. Done."

"Not the slightest chance you could work it out?" Jayne furrowed her brow.

"None."

"Dammit," Jayne swore and plunked down in a chair beside the worktable. "Now I'm going to have to get a tattoo."

Eden stopped what she was doing and glanced at Jayne. "What on earth are you talking about?"

"I lost a wager to Ashley."

"A wager?"

"I bet her that Sarah Armstrong and I could make a match between you and Alec."

"Excuse me?" Eden sank her hands on her hips.

"Sarah sent Alec into the boutique with the hopes you two would spark and, boy, did you."

"It was a setup?" Her voice came out high and reedy.

"And then I got Ashley to call in sick the day of Jill and Randy's wedding shower so you would have to go out to Connecticut to deliver the basket."

"You were behind that." Eden clenched her hands into fists. Jayne was supposed to be her friend. How could she have manipulated her?

"Now don't get upset, please. You have to know we both had your best interests at heart. Sarah realized Alec wasn't really as dedicated to bachelorhood as he claimed to be and all he needed was to meet the right woman. While I hated seeing you so cloistered because of those scars. I knew if anyone could see past your physical imperfections, it was Alec."

"Well, that's where you were wrong," Eden said, surprised to hear the strength of her bitterness. "He did turn away from me because of the scars."

"No!" Jayne looked appalled.

"Yes. In fact, he couldn't get away from me fast enough after I finally let him see me completely naked."

Jayne sucked in a deep breath. "Oh, Eden, I'm so sorry. I never planned for you to get hurt. All Sarah and I wanted was for you guys to be happy."

"Your heart might have been in the right place, Jayne, but I did get hurt."

And then the tears she'd been denying for two

weeks burst forth in a torrent and she found herself enveloped in Jayne's arms.

"Shh. There, there. It'll be all right."

The severity of the sobs racking her body told her she hadn't fully dealt with what had happened. She'd stayed busy and swept her emotions under the rug. She would survive this. She would forget about Alec. But in the meantime, she needed to get as far away from Manhattan and the painful memories as she could get.

ALEC RETURNED from Norway the following Monday. He trudged into the office, still trying to get his mind around the notion that Uncle Mac was getting married.

"You okay?" Holden asked, concern pinching his forehead in a frown.

"Fine." Listlessly he picked up the mail from Holden's in basket and thumbed through it. For some inexplicable and illogical reason he checked the return addresses to see if he'd gotten anything from Eden.

"You don't look fine. You look sick. Usually you come back from your trips hyped up and full of energy."

"Not this time."

How could he begin to tell Holden the jump from Kjerag had been as boring as watching paint dry, when he didn't even understand it himself?

"Randy and Jill are in your office. They just returned from Tahiti and they broke into your champagne. I'll order more.''

Alec shook his head. ''Don't bother. I've got nothing to celebrate.''

Holden's frown deepened. ''Are you sure you're okay?''

''Why do you keep asking me that?''

''Where's your lively stride, your boisterous grin? I'm supposed to be the dour one around here.''

''Can't a guy be quiet once in a while?''

''You?'' Holden snorted.

Glaring at his assistant, Alec turned on his heels and went into his office. He found Randy and Jill perched on the love seat, locked in the throes of a soulful kiss.

''Ahem.'' He cleared his throat.

They ignored him.

''Ahem,'' he said again, much louder this time.

Jill giggled and Randy finally broke the kiss.

''I take it the honeymoon was a rousing success.'' Alec arched an eyebrow.

''You have no idea how rousing,'' Randy said to Alec, but his gaze was zeroed in on Jill's face. She couldn't seem to take her eyes off him, either. They looked so radiantly happy together a peculiar feeling had Alec rolling his eyes. Could they be any more of a romantic cliché?

Why, Alec Ramsey, you're jealous.

Jealous of a married couple? No way, no how. He was free, single and loving it.

Oh hell, who was he kidding? He was so jealous it's a wonder his hair hadn't turned green.

First Randy. Now Mac. What was the point of being a footloose bachelor if all your buddies were happily paired up? Where did that leave him?

All alone.

The urge to drown his loneliness in activity swept over him, but he realized his old coping mechanisms were no longer effective. He couldn't keep running away from the truth, couldn't keep cloaking his emotions with planning and playing. He couldn't keep lying to himself about his feelings.

He was in love with Eden Montgomery. He'd never met anyone like her. Sweet yet sassy. Silly yet sublime. He thought of the smell of her hair, the touch of her fingertips against his skin, the taste of those small pert lips and he knew he simply could not live the rest of his life without her.

But what about the magazine? demanded the macho voice that had convinced him marriage was for suckers.

To hell with the magazine, roared the new Alec. If his readers couldn't deal with a married man at the helm of *Single Guy,* if falling in love meant his reputation in his social milieu was kablewy, then so what? He would find another way to make a living. He could get a whole new circle of friends.

What he couldn't get was another woman like Eden. A woman who engaged him mentally, emotionally and sexually the way she did. She made him want to commit. She made him want to shout to the world he'd been wrong. He was in love and he wasn't ashamed of it any longer.

That simple realization set him free. Every tender emotion he'd ever suppressed bubbled up inside him. He wanted her as his wife. He wanted her as the mother of his children. He wanted to grow old with her. He wanted to spend the rest of his days trying to please her as much as she pleased him.

He had to go to her. Now.

Alec turned and headed for the door.

"Hey," Randy said. "Where you going?"

"To see Eden."

"I thought you two broke up," Randy said.

"We did, but I aim to fix that."

Jill raised a hand. "Alec, she's not in Manhattan."

"What?"

"We stopped by the shop when we got into the city. Her assistant Ashley told us she's gone on a spiritual retreat to get her head together. Apparently you did quite a number on her."

"What?" Stunned, Alec stared at Jill, the pain in his chest so unbearable he wanted to jump out of an airplane, but then he reminded himself that was no way to deal with his feelings. He had to ride this out.

"Ashley said Eden is convinced you dumped her because of her burn scars."

"What? But that's ridiculous. Eden is the one who dumped me...I..." Alec stopped and closed his eyes.

He remembered how he'd acted the morning after their last night together, how he'd been so panicked over the intimate feelings she'd stirred in him that he'd raced back to the city and left her standing outside Wickedly Wonderful all alone.

God, he was an ass, a jerk, and an idiot to boot. He had to get her back, beg her forgiveness and swear to her that if she would give him a second chance he would spend the rest of his days proving exactly how much he loved and adored her.

"Where is she? How can I find her?"

Jill shook her head. "Ashley wouldn't tell us. She said Eden doesn't want to be disturbed."

"I have to see her."

"I gotta say, it's going to take a lot to convince her that you've changed," Jill said.

Randy nodded. "It's going to take a grand gesture, man. Something irreversible, so she knows you mean business."

Alec clenched his jaw, the mental cogs in his brain whirling. Only one thing would truly convince her. He knew what he had to do.

15

EDEN BLASTED Gloria Gaynor's "I Will Survive" on her Walkman headphones as she shopped in the rustic convenience store outside Sedona, Arizona. She walked down the narrow aisles, bopping her head in time to the music and filling the blue plastic basket slung over her arm with goodies not allowed at the Sacred Health Tranquility Spa.

A raging urge for chocolate had forced her to defy her New Age spiritual guide Arnold Red Bear to sneak down the mountain for her fix. She tossed a box of chocolate-chip cookies into the basket along with a six-pack of cola, two fudge-nut brownies and three devil dogs.

She'd spent the past week finding her center and cleansing her aura. And while she'd learned more than she'd ever cared to know about crystals and chakras and color therapy she wasn't any closer to serenity than the day she'd fled Manhattan, simply because she couldn't stop thinking about Alec.

In a last-ditch effort to banish him from her mind, she decided to give in to her hurt feelings and anger by listening to Gloria and overdosing on chocolate.

Defiance. Might not be as pretty as serenity, but she felt better than she had felt since arriving in Arizona.

She hummed along with the tune between mouthfuls of a Snickers bar, while waiting in line behind a group of Japanese tourists at the checkout counter.

Okay, so she'd taken a risk and it hadn't worked out. She gotten battered and bruised, but, by gosh, she *would* survive.

Not to mention, she'd had some pretty great sex with Alec and that was nothing to sneeze at. So what if he hadn't fallen in love with her the way she'd fallen in love with him. She wouldn't be the first woman in history to go gaga over a Peter Pan man and live to regret it.

And he *had* made her feel special, at least for a little while. What more could she ask for?

That thought caused her throat to tighten and her heart to go all gooey.

Knock it off, Eden.

To distract herself from the merry-go-round of what-if questions that had been dogging her ever since the day after Randy and Jill's wedding, Eden perused the magazine rack beside the counter.

Cosmo. Time. Reader's Digest. Single Guy.

Single Guy?

She stopped noshing on the Snickers and her knees went weak. They carried *Single Guy* in the wilds of rustic Arizona?

But that wasn't the shocking part. What riveted her attention was the picture on the front cover.

A tuxedoed Alec Ramsey, looking impossibly

handsome with his daredevil grin and his sexily disheveled dark hair, stared back at her. In the photograph, his hand was extended and he held a black velvet box cracked open to reveal a stunning diamond ring.

She blinked, shook her head and stepped toward the rack for a better look.

Alec? With an engagement ring in his hand gracing the cover of his magazine?

What in the hell?

Then she read the headline and lost her breath.

Eden Montgomery, Will You Marry Me?

ALEC PACED HIS OFFICE. The latest issue of *Single Guy* had been on the stands for two days and still no word from Eden. In the past forty-eight hours he'd called Wickedly Wonderful at least three dozen times and Ashley was beginning to lose patience with him.

"Look, dude," she said in exasperation before hanging up on him. "If Eden wants to contact you, she knows where you are."

But what happens if she doesn't want to contact me? He thought as he cradled the receiver, a sick feeling curling in his belly. Ah hell, he'd burned his bridges asking her to marry him on the front cover of his magazine. Which of course, had been the point. No going back now.

The phones in his office had been ringing off the hook. Some readers called to express their anger, telling him he was a sellout, but surprisingly, he'd discovered a lot of supporters as well. Many readers had confessed that while they liked being single right now, they hoped someday to find that someone special.

Old girlfriends had called, as well as his mother and sisters. Several television stations wanted to interview him and a well-known aging playboy had offered to buy *Single Guy* if he was interested in selling.

Yesterday, Mac had shown up with a magnum of champagne and a smiling Sophie on his arm, but when Mac proposed a toast to "seeing what was right in front of your face," Alec had been unable to swallow his drink.

Until he knew how Eden felt about him, he couldn't celebrate.

The distractions, which he once would have embraced as a way to keep himself from dwelling on the situation, now simply irritated him. He didn't care what his readers thought. He didn't want to be interviewed. He put off the prospective buyer and brushed off the premature congratulations. Only one person mattered and he was on tenterhooks until he heard from her.

Dammit, where was she?

What if the retreat she'd gone to was so reclusive she hadn't seen the magazine?

What if she had seen it and she was mortified?

What if she didn't love him the way he loved her?

What if...ah hell, where was a worry stone when you needed one?

He shoved his fingers through his hair, stalked the length of his office for the seven millionth time and stopped beside the bookcase where the hourglass she'd given him sat.

Okay. This was it. He needed a sign.

Alec took the hourglass to his desk and flipped it over. If Eden called before the last grain of sand ran through the neck of the hourglass, then it was good news. If not, he'd just made a romantic fool of himself in front of three hundred thousand loyal readers and anyone else in America who happened to see the cover.

Morosely Alec plopped down in his chair, propped his elbows on the desk, dropped his chin into his open palms and stared at the hourglass. Each grain of sand that trickled through the neck took Eden just a little bit farther away from him.

Patience.

The word came to him from the ether.

Let's take it slow, sixty-minute man.

The sound of Eden's voice filled his ears and he was transported back to the night she first introduced the hourglass into their lovemaking and encouraged him to slow down and take things nice and easy.

He sighed. God, how he needed her to keep him in line. How had he lived so long without her?

Trickle, trickle, trickle.

Alec focused on the sand and allowed it to mesmerize him. He was going to do absolutely nothing for the next hour.

And after that...

He shook his head. He couldn't think any farther down the road past that last grain of sand.

Seconds passed, then minutes. He stared at the hourglass, never looking away, mentally willing the phone to ring.

Call me, Eden. Call me now.

Trickle, trickle, trickle.

Fifteen minutes. Twenty. Thirty.

He shifted in his seat. Every time he heard the phone ring at Holden's desk, he tensed, waiting for his assistant to dispatch the call into his office.

But the call never came.

He knew it was illogical to put such a restrictive stipulation on a one-hour span of time. He knew she could easily call five minutes after the sand ran out or not at all. The absurdity of it was a symptom of his emotional stress.

As he watched the last grain of sand slide through the hourglass, his body went limp. He was as exhausted as if he'd spent the day digging ditches.

Unfortunately, he had his answer.

Face it, Ramsey. It's over.

He pushed back from the desk and raised his head and that's when he saw her.

Standing in the doorway of his office, one shoulder leaned insouciantly against the doorframe, dressed in the black body suit she'd worn the night they made love in the Ferrari, the familiar black skirt topping the body suit, the same duster pulled provocatively over her lovely breasts.

Eden.

He rose to his feet, his knees watery, his heart ka-booming like a ten-piece timpani band.

"Hey there, sixty-minute man," her voice, low and seductive, wrapped around him.

He couldn't speak, could only stare and stare and stare. Was she real? Or simply a figment of his over-wrought imagination.

Her hair was loose and cascading about her shoulders in a splendid tumble. Her lips were painted a luscious shade of red. She'd made a necklace of the worry stone and it hung at the hollow of her throat. She looked poised and relaxed and absolutely gorgeous.

In her hand, she held a copy of *Single Guy*.

"Still a fan of the grand gestures, I see." Her tone was teasing, but the light in her eyes was anything but frivolous.

"Uh-huh," was all he could manage.

"Sort of backed yourself into a corner with this one."

"It's a corner I want to be backed into."

"Are you sure?"

To hell with this. He had to touch her, hold her, kiss her. Purposely he stalked around the desk and headed straight toward her.

She met his gaze and held her ground.

"What happened to Mr. I'll-Never-Get-Married?"

"He grew up," Alec growled, pulling her into his arms and over the threshold.

He saw half his employees peeking down the corridor at them before he slammed the door closed with his foot and dragged her flush against his chest.

"Just like that?" She looked up at him, her eyes ablaze with passion.

"No. Not just like that. I grew up because of you."

She pulled away from him and stepped back. "I find it hard to believe you could change so easily."

"Believe me, sweetheart, it's been anything but easy. I tried to forget you. Lord knows, I tried, but I can't get you out of my head or out of my heart."

Uncertainty flitted across her face. He watched her reach up and touch the worry stone with one hand while at the same time laying the palm of her other hand across her abdomen.

"You're sure it's me you want?"

"I've never been more sure of anything in my life."

"You could have any woman you want. Models. Actresses. Why me?"

"Other than the fact that I'm wildly in love with you?"

"Uh-huh."

"Because you keep me guessing. Because you make me examine my motives. Because you're both sexy and sweet. Determined and yet yielding. Strong-minded but flexible. I'm crazy about the dichotomy that is you. But most of all, I love you because you bring out the best in me."

"But I'm scarred, Alec. Flawed."

He snagged her around the waist. "I gave thanks for those scars because they've made you the woman you are today. I think you're perfect just the way you are, Eden. Don't you get it?" He tapped her chest over her heart with an index finger. "I love what's in here."

Tears misted her eyes. "But the night after you saw me naked, you barely spoke to me. You couldn't get me back to Manhattan quickly enough. Until then, you'd been pushing to extend our affair and after you saw me naked…poof. You disappeared."

"Sweetheart, it wasn't the scars. You've got a body made for loving." He ran his hands over her body to prove to her exactly how much he desired her. "I ran off because *I* got scared. That night when I looked into your eyes I realized for the first time exactly how much I loved you. The feelings I had were so overwhelming I tried to deny them."

"Really?"

"Really. I mean here I was, a guy who'd spent his life playing the field, avoiding commitment, building his reputation and his livelihood on being a bachelor and I was stone-cold terrified to realize I'd been *wrong*. I thought love meant the death of romance. I thought marriage meant the fun was over. Randy tried to tell me what I was missing, but I just wasn't listening. I couldn't understand until I'd been there myself. I let my father's death and my uncle's experiences guide me when I should have listened to my own heart."

"But how do you know for sure?"

"I know for sure because when I tried to do the things I used to do. I no longer enjoyed any of it. Without you, everything was empty, meaningless. I realized I'd been filling my life with activity in order to block my true feelings.''

''But aren't you afraid of being tied down? Of losing your freedom?''

''Honey, you give my life meaning and direction. Your tether keeps me from flying away. Tie me up, tie me down, just tie the knot with me.''

Eden stared into his eyes and what she saw reflected in those dark gray depths moved her deeply and allowed her to release the remaining threads of doubt. His commitment to her wasn't frivolous or impulsive or poorly thought out. He meant what he was saying.

''You're serious.'' Her pulse rate, which had been spiking through the roof ever since she'd jumped on the plane in Arizona, finally slowed to a relaxed, comfortable rhythm as her man dipped his head and kissed away every last worst-case scenario.

''I love you, Eden. Now, forever and always. This isn't a game. It's real. You can count on that. You can count on me.''

He said exactly what she needed to hear most. The little girl who'd endured an unstable childhood, the young woman who'd been scarred by burns, the sexual novice who'd found the courage to explore her femininity even after being cruelly spurned, felt the old fears shed like a chrysalis. Eden nodded, accepting the precious gift she knew this man did not give lightly.

''Oh, Alec,'' she breathed and melted into him. ''I love you, too.''

Epilogue

"SATIN ROPES?"

"Check."

"Peacock feathers?"

"Check."

"Worry stone?"

"Check."

"Hourglass?"

"Check."

"Black lace stockings and matching garter belt?"

"Check and double check."

"Condoms ribbed for her pleasure?"

Eden licked her lips and winked at him. "As if I'd forget *those*."

Alec gazed at his wife sitting on the counter at Wickedly Wonderful, playfully swinging her legs and stocking their vacation basket with enough sex toys to keep them occupied for a month. The provocative glow in her eyes caught him low in the belly and flamed his passion the way it always did.

How on earth had he ever once believed that loving one woman for the rest of his life would be boring? In twelve months of marriage he'd enjoyed more revolutionary sex and romantic spontaneity with Eden then he'd experienced in twenty-seven years as a single guy. Why hadn't anyone told him what he'd been missing out on?

Your married friends tried, remember. You were just too pigheaded to listen.

"So where are we going this time?" he asked, trying to get a peek at the travel brochure she had tucked in her cleavage.

Every six weeks Eden arranged for a secret weekend getaway. She understood his need for stimulation and variety and he loved her for her efforts. Sometimes the getaway was in their own apartment, like the time she'd turned their bedroom into a Mexican bordello. She'd met him at the door with a lime wedge in her mouth, a bottle of tequila in one hand and wearing nothing but a serape.

Six weeks ago they'd gone back to the Grand Duchess and Lola, of the hundred-dollar hand job, had returned to work her magic. Alec grinned, remembering.

This time, however, Alec knew Eden was planning something big. The size of the basket was a major giveaway, plus, it was their one-year wedding anniversary. She'd cajoled him into taking a week off, leaving Randy to oversee their newest publication *Adventures in Marriage*. They'd just launched the first issue and it had been an unqualified success. Holden was helming *Single Guy* since Alec had made him managing editor.

Ashley and Jayne had been recruited to keep Wickedly Wonderful running. Everything was set for seven blissful days in paradise.

"Guess," Eden teased, waving the brochures out of his reach.

"Someplace tropical. Warm beaches, umbrella drinks, lots of time spent hiding out in our own little grass hut."

"Nope."

"Paris?"

She shook her head, her chestnut curls bobbing seductively about her shoulders.

"Don't tell me. You've booked us in the Sacred Health Tranquility Spa in Sedona."

"Not hardly."

"I give up."

"My baskets have been so popular Spice-Up-Your-Love-Life is giving us a free cruise."

"No kidding. Where to?"

"Alaska."

"But that's cold. I want to go somewhere I can get you naked."

"Oh, I'll be naked all right. Under a mound of furs. Ever made love in an igloo?"

"Can't say I have."

"Ooh, another first time for us. And of course there's always the heated hot tub in our stateroom."

"Now you're talking." He moved to kiss her. She wrapped her legs around his waist and he lifted her off the counter. His body tingled with anticipation for all the adventures that lay ahead of them. She sucked his neck, raked her fingers through his hair.

He reached for the buttons on her blouse, but Eden pulled away with a teasing grin. "No time. The ship starts boarding in an hour."

"Minx. You adore getting me riled up, then dragging it out."

"And you love the torture." She unclamped her legs from his waist and slid her feet to the floor. "Grab the suitcases and let's hit the road."

Eden reached for the basket, but Alec put out a hand to stop her.

"You know," he said, reaching for the condoms. "What's the worst that could happen if we were to leave these behind?"

Eden inhaled sharply. "What are you saying, playboy?"

"I'm saying I want babies, Eden. Lots and lots of babies."

"Are you sure?"

He saw excitement flare bright in her eyes and he knew it was the right thing to do. "I've only been surer of one thing in my life."

"And what's that?"

"Marrying you."

"You're such a flirt."

"And you love that about me." He ran his tongue over her lip and she sighed. "Now about those babies…"

"The ship's boarding," she murmured weakly, kissing him back.

He skimmed his hands up under her skirt and tenderly touched her scar. "Yes, but it probably won't sail for at least two hours, right?"

"Hmm."

"Flip over that hourglass, woman," he breathed into her mouth.

"My sixty-minute man."

"Your sixty-minute man is going to give you a baby. What do you have to say to that?"

"Bring it on."

He peeled off her panties and then climbed up on the counter beside her. Their breaths came in hot, measured gasps as their kisses heated up.

And then, Alec gave pleasure to the woman he loved with all his heart. He took her slow, soft and easy and it was sinfully, wickedly...*wonderful.*

HARLEQUIN® *Blaze*™

In L.A., nothing remains confidential for long...

KISS & TELL

Don't miss

Tori Carrington's

exciting new miniseries featuring four
twentysomething friends—
and the secrets they *don't* keep.

Look for:

#105—NIGHT FEVER
October 2003

#109—FLAVOR OF THE MONTH
November 2003

#113—JUST BETWEEN US...
December 2003

Available wherever Harlequin books are sold.

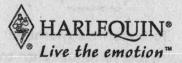

HARLEQUIN®
Live the emotion™

An offer you can't afford to refuse!

High-valued coupons for upcoming books

**A sneak peek at Harlequin's newest line—
Harlequin Flipside™**

**Send away for a hardcover by *New York Times*
bestselling author Debbie Macomber**

How can you get all this?

Buy four Harlequin or Silhouette books during
October–December 2003, fill out the form below and send
the form and four proofs of purchase (cash register receipts)
to the address below.

I accept this amazing offer!
Send me a coupon booklet:

Name (PLEASE PRINT)

Address   Apt. #

City   State/Prov.   Zip/Postal Code
                                        098 KIN DXHT

Please send this form, along with your cash register receipts
as proofs of purchase, to:

In the U.S.:
Harlequin Coupon Booklet Offer, P.O. Box 9071, Buffalo, NY 14269-9071

In Canada:
Harlequin Coupon Booklet Offer, P.O. Box 609, Fort Erie, Ontario L2A 5X3

**Allow 4–6 weeks for delivery. Offer expires December 31, 2003.
Offer good only while quantities last.**

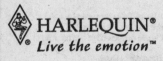

Visit us at www.eHarlequin.com

Q42003

HARLEQUIN®
Blaze™

COMING NEXT MONTH

#109 FLAVOR OF THE MONTH Tori Carrington
Kiss & Tell, Bk. 2

Four friends. Countless secrets… Pastry shop owner Reilly Cudowski
has spent most of her life squelching her secret cravings. But when delicious
Benjamin Kane shows up, she can't help indulging a little.
Only, the more she has Ben, the more she wants. So what else can
Reilly do but convince him that a lifetime of desserts can be even sweeter…?

#110 OVER THE EDGE Jeanie London

After ten years of patient planning, Mallory Hunt finally has Jake Trinity
right where she wants him. He's contracted her security expertise, and
while she's at it, she'll push *his* sensual edges. Their long-ago first meeting—
and its steamy kiss—changed her life, and now it's time
for payback. But Mallory doesn't count on the intense heat between
them or the fact she doesn't *want* this to end!

#111 YOURS TO SEDUCE Karen Anders
Women Who Dare, Bk. 2

When firefighter Lana Dempsey finally tackles fellow firefighter
Sean O'Neill in the…showers, it's a five-alarm blaze. Stripped of their uni-
forms, it's what Lana's always wanted. Having had a crush on Sean since
forever, she'd never been brave enough to do anything about it. Until the
bet she'd made with her girlfriends gives her the courage
to finally squelch that burning desire for Sean!

#112 ANYTHING GOES… Debbi Rawlins

Seven days of sun, sand and sex, sex, sex! That's exactly what
Carly Saunders needs—anonymous sex…and lots of it. She has
one week of sin before she heads home to a teaching job—and her
place as the pastor's daughter. So she's going to make this week count.
Only, she never dreams she'll meet Rick, her best friend growing up.
Or that he'll have the same agenda…

Visit us at www.eHarlequin.com